Lux Prismatica

Dreams of Recursive Reincarnation

Story 1: Chosen Colors

Story 2: Render

Story 3: Dolly 23

Lux Prismatica is a collection of the original works **Render** and **Dolly 23** by Joshua Lee Andrew Jones and **Chosen Colors** by Mark C Frankel.

Cover design by Alexander Sapountzis

Published by Wayward Raven Media, LLC.
Copyright 2022

First edition: 2022
Subjects: Science Fiction

ISBN: 979-8-9868513-0-3

Printed in the United States of America

More works by Wayward Raven Media

- ➢ Horsemen
- ➢ Signed C: The Missing
- ➢ The Ascendant
- ➢ Infusion
- ➢ The Cycle
- ➢ Damn Heroes: Volumes 1-4
- ➢ Ominous Odes
- ➢ The Cell
- ➢ Percy: A Children's Adventure Story

All available on https://waywardraven.com

Foreword

In the long ago, Mark Frankel and I bonded over shared interests. This included world mythologies. I had been writing novels but a conversation inspired a joint interest and a collaboration arose. This was writing stage plays with fantasy elements during the days when you had to send bulky submissions in the mail.

Though that did not work out, it did cement a partnership in developing stories. Our love of comic books brought us to the desire to write them. A little nudge by a comic book industry professional put us on that path. A very long and difficult path. In 2012, we put out two comic books and exhibited at New York Comic Con. There, a third member officially joined: Alex Sapountzis. Then, the company Wayward Raven Media took flight to strange and wonderful adventures.

I never stopped writing novels, short stories, or poetry but they were on the back burner. No longer. This is why we bring you my novella titled **Render** and a short story titled **Dolly 23**. Both set in the same universe but from alternate points of view. We convinced Mark to add a story as well so **Lux Prismatica** was born. I hope you enjoy the scifi tales.

Ars longa, vitae brevis.

~ Joshua Lee Andrew Jones

Intro, forward, backward, preamble, lead-in…whatever.

I usually skip these things and go right to the story. You won't offend me if you do the same. They bore me. I mean, who really cares why the author wrote something? Or why the person chosen to introduce the story was picked out of a handful of other patsies. So seriously, go ahead and get to the meat of things. I mean it. Go on. Skip ahead. Piss off. Begone!

No? Still there, hmm? Okay, but don't say I didn't warn you…

So how the hell did I end up here? I mean, not just existentially (your guess is as good as mine on that account. Some form of cosmic accident seems appropriately funny to me), but why in all of the Cthuluan horrors am I included in this compendium? And why am I writing a prologue? On a side note, spell check had a devil of a time with the word Cthuluan, so I felt compelled to write it again. It wanted me to correct it to "Italian." Go ahead and try it with your PC and see what results you get.

Well to answer the question you didn't ask and likely don't care to obtain the answer to, Josh had a marvelous story. And then he wrote another wondrous story to go with it, set in the former's universe. And we were going to publish the first story, but in one of our weekly sessions we had an idea to include a few more stories and put it out as a compilation. Therefore, I volunteered to write a short story. Alex said he might add some artwork. Pretty straightforward really. Fairly mundane. I mean, I DID **warn you**.

And so there you have it. That's it. Simple. So are you sated? Did I answer the question sufficiently and we can just move on to the stories...ow! Hey, stop! Ouch! Okay, fine, I'll write more...just...just stop zapping me with that blasted cattle prod. Zounds.

So as I was saying, Josh had a marvelous story. I mean, I knew it was a marvelous story because I read it. And edited it too, so any typos you encounter are likely my fault entirely. Apologies. And then he had another marvelous story. I read and edited that one as well. Again, apologies for any errors you encounter.

Knowing that Josh had not one, but two spectacular stories, I knew I had to write something complimentary. Something to fit with his theme. Something amazing, nay sublime! A story that would go down in the annals of storytelling as one of the great works, mayhaps besting The Odyssey or Shakespeare's combined works or The Bible even! I'll write the Greatest. Tale. Ever. Told!!!!!!

Ahem. Excuse me. I imagine I was going on there for a bit like a comic book supervillain? Hmm, I do that sometimes. Frankly, I blame the deathray I created. Well, intended deathray. Mainly it annoys pigeons. Side effects of using it are increased importance (not to be confused with impotence, you ninny), delusions of adequacy, and occasional "gassiness." I enjoy the last one the least.

Unfortunately, I fear the story I wrote fell well short of my goal. Nonetheless, my intentions were pure. It was, quite frankly, a difficult story to write and still keep to my original premise. It surprised me how formidable it is to write a tale without describing noises or using sounds of any kind. As you can imagine, it makes a huge impact on dialogue. I hope by sharing this information with you the story isn't spoiled. Of course, I will take a moment again to note that I did tell you to skip this session. It isn't my fault you are clearly stubborn.

I think you'll find that perspective is quite important in my tale (well all three tales, frankly). Part of that is what you might have already gathered from some of the above statements. I think you will also find it will examine cultural norms. I won't say much more about that. I'd rather you experience it for yourself (I only like to spoil so much), but I will say that I feel they fit well with the spirit of Josh's tales. Additionally, the Sci-Fi genre seems to fit perfectly for all three stories in this compendium.

So is that sufficient? Have I satisfied your word quotient in these opening remarks? Slaked your curiosity? Provided you the solace required to get on to the meat of the matter? Well, if I haven't then it is no one's fault but your own. If you are left wanting by these comments, then I will simply repeat for a final time, *I told you so.*

And in case you are wondering, yes, I wrote this whole thing in an English accent. I don't possess an English accent, I simply wrote it in that voice. Or at least that of a pedantic college professor. Perhaps both. Missed that then, did you? Well, shame on you. Go back and read it again properly. Wanker.

Yours Truly,

Chief Debater, Repeated Rulebreaker, Frequent Agitator and Occasional Scofflaw

Mark C. Frankel

Chosen Colors

By

Mark C. Frankel

Edited by Joshua L. A. Jones

Chosen Colors

Biborka Ninad allowed the hot wind to wash over her. Her bristles stood at attention along her exposed areas. The nearly invisible hairs catching innumerable grains of sands as the light breeze from the desert kissed her. The thousands of whiskery cilium were normally soft but a day in these elements meant she was destined for either a long soak in the cleansing pools or a vigorous grooming with the munskrii brush. Until then, the invading particles would make her feel vaguely amorous. It wasn't an undesirable state, but it certainly wasn't ideal for one of *The Chroma* to experience without others of her kind.

A cowl encircled her head and covered her mouth, keeping the sand from some of her more sensitive areas, but it did little for her exposed appendages. Large circular glass disks attached to her face with a suction putty kept the grains from her eyes. She was unable to wear glasses like the denizens of the planet did, although she could have attached their type of goggles if she desired. The strap would have affixed it perfectly around her head, but it tended to press on her rear dorsals, eventually causing her a throbbing pain in the areas where they were bent along the base of her skull. That made the suction glass her best option.

The sun almost finished its descent, but the heat remained. In fact, it would likely last until the yellow orb rose again. That didn't bother Biborka. Her physiology was made to tolerate extreme heat. She understood that was why her people had settled in an area that was intolerable to most other species, including the humans whose hubris compelled them to found a city here that would perish if not for the immense wall clogging the waterway and powering it. Many of her kind scoffed at the frail creature's arrogance. Not Biborka.

Involuntarily, her cheeks puffed in and out in two quick bursts. Containing her excitement was difficult and she chastised herself for allowing it to show. At least she hadn't let them flair an apricot, or worse, a violent red. Instead, she held fast to her natural lavender. That might prove difficult as the evening wore on, but at least she could prevent shows of exuberance before the adventure had even begun.

If she was being fair, she might have cut herself at least a modicum of slack. She was, after all, entering the city limits on her own for the first time. Everything here was so bright, so vibrant. The sun still hung in the sky, but the lights blared as if it were the darkest of evenings. Strobes, neons, multicolored blasts surrounded her everywhere on that main thoroughfare.

Biborka was mildly concerned about The Sickness. This was when it often set in for her kind. The garishness, this embarrassment of colors and frenetic images, was known to strike down even the most sober-minded of her people. She was young though and certain only those unprepared for what they were to experience would fall victim. Not Biborka. She had prepared for this trip with hours watching their television programs. On those screens no image ever lasted longer than seconds. If she could watch such programming tirelessly, she should be more than equipped to withstand some flashing lights.

No one knew Biborka had made this trip. If she had her way, she would be back before anyone could find out too. One night in Las Vegas was exciting, but she was certain she would be back before the day broke. It was her turn to prove she could withstand the allure of the human's society, not because others of her people had done so, and returned to brag about it, but for herself. Biborka could feel the pull of these simian's reckless and showy ways. She **needed** to explore it for herself.

As she understood it, the chief oddity amongst the humans was something they called sound or possibly noise. It was a communication tool for them. Her peers had spoken of it, but until three cycles ago, none of her people claimed to have experienced it. To the horror of many of The Chroma, that was no longer true.

Although Biborka's immediate family structure avowed it was nonsense, many of The Chroma, and a few of her relatives, now sported an unusual augmentation they claimed allowed them to experience waves caused by clashing objects or other noises. They called them ears. The Highest Chroma called them nonsense. They claimed those who had these horrors attached to their heads by human surgery had simply lived in too close proximity to mankind for too long and had begun adopting their ways. Biborka was skeptical. She could feel the waves crash over her chest and down her body even now as she walked amongst their glowing metropolis. It seemed clear to her there was something to these tales.

Biborka ambled along the sidewalk of the garish city. As cars raged by her on the clogged street, Biborka couldn't deny the crash of some kind of wave striking her. She could almost feel each vehicle as it passed, some a fair amount closer than she would have liked. She had been warned to be careful here. The locals were not often friendly to her kind. The visitors viewed The Chroma as oddities and snapped photographs to share with their friends. And she had heard tales of those that had gone even further.

As she walked, Biborka could see the thinly veiled expressions on the human faces. Fear. Anger. Curiosity. Most didn't bother to hide it. They opened their maws and waggled their lips. Sometimes their tongue as well. She refused to respond. Did they expect her to converse with them? Sometimes she would puff her cheeks or flush a red or orange reflexively. It didn't matter. Humans didn't communicate in Chromalist. At least none of the ones she had encountered. In any case, she didn't think any would bother to learn, even if they were physically capable.

Biborka found a building that towered over many of the others. The lights here flashed brighter and more frequently than many of the others. It was as good a place to go in as any other. It helped that she saw another of The Chroma enter through a revolving door. She hadn't been quick enough to see if the patron had implants. Perhaps she could catch up and find out.

As Biborka followed through the spinning door, she found herself confronted by a crowd of sorts on the other end. Her cheeks flushed a bright red of annoyance. Fargut! Where did her brethren go?

Scanning the crowd, she saw no sign of any other member of her kind. A spike of adrenaline burst in her chest. What if this establishment wasn't friendly to her kind? She felt her cheeks change their color again, this time a deep maroon of embarrassment and fear. She didn't belong here. She should be home in her Gorpa that smelled vaguely of cooked sprouts, the remains of a burned cistroon and the cleansing bathing oils she favored. Not in this blinding din that reeked of sweat and overserved beverages, some of which she was certain had spilled and were now forever entwined with the carpeted floor.

Biborka shut her eyes tightly. It didn't stop the flashing auras from penetrating her vision, but it did dampen their effects. She inhaled deeply once. And then again. She could handle this, they were just lights. Certainly nothing as special as the brilliant colors she could make on her own. Another deep inhale.

She opened her eyes. Luck was on Biborka's side. Directly in her field of vision, across a room full of flashing lights on machinery she didn't recognize, stood another of her kind. His blue feathering marked him as an elder of The Chroma. And he did indeed have implants on either side of his head. Finally, here was someone who could answer her questions.

*   *   *

Id felt a Green first. Then Yellow. Somehow they were intertwined or combined, but mostly it felt Green. The Yellow was more distant. Id realized that they were separate things. They appeared to merge in Id's vision and then separate. The Yellow retreated while the Green became encompassing. Id was hungry. The Green surrounded Id and Id ate greedily. Id didn't know what it was, but Id knew hunger. And Id sated itself with the Green. Id felt a color. Yes, Id would be Orange. And so Id became Orange. And then Id descended back into the black.

*   *   *

Biborka skirted the throng of humans the best she could, only bumping into one. It was a male of the species. The thing flared its nostrils and drew its eyes down the length of her body before turning away and continuing on its path. She flared a deliberate apologetical light pink a moment after he turned his back, just in case anyone was observing her.

She worried that the brief incident would deviate Biborka from her course, but her fears were unfounded. The elder male had settled down at one of the human's game stations with a large stack of tokens. It appeared he intended to be there for some while.

She suppressed a desire to approach him directly, to swiftly swoop in and ask query after query in a demanding fashion. In Biborka's experience, many older males would forgive preadolescent Oranges such behavior, but her purple feathering marked her as capable of patiently observing at least some basic protocols. At this stage of her life, it was expected of Biborka to at a minimum acquaint herself with another before barraging them with questions.

Uncertainly, Boborka observed the Blue from three or four meters almost directly behind him. She watched his back as he picked up a stack of markers, stood, and distributed ten or twelve of them across the board. Then he sat down and waited, watching the spinning ball until it fell. He must have chosen wisely as his stack of markers increased.

Biborka circled him slightly, just enough to get a better look at his visage and carriage. She did not yet dare go any closer. Much of his blue feathering had fallen out, leaving wispy reminders of the plumage. There were a few stubborn tufts still clinging to his scalp, each one appearing long and stringy. He wore glasses like many of these humans, likely due to a degenerative eye condition she understood occurred in many Blues. Instead of the suction-based glass like Biborka's individual panes, his were supported on the sides where the frame rested upon his aural implants. In humans they are called ears, she reminded herself.

Scars ran down the Blue's scalp right above where the implants had been inserted into his skull. They were not fresh and appeared to have healed long ago, possibly years. A jolt went through Biborka's body as she realized this Blue must have been one of the original implantees. One had to look very closely for scars on newer surgeries. The Blue would have all manner of knowledge about this "hearing" the humans claim to possess. Her cheeks swirled a rainbow of colors, revealing her sudden amazement to any capable of reading them.

And the Blue was capable. In that moment, he turned ninety degrees to his right, placing her along the perimeter of his vision. Biborka froze as he paused to stare out into the crowd. He feigned as if he would turn back towards his game, but instead drew a deep breath and turned further to his right to center Biborka directly in his sight.

The Blue tapped his right implant and inclined his head in that direction, all the while looking at her. His cheeks puffed exactly five quick times and then held steady on one final puff. They colored from an annoyed yellow-orange to a pale green before settling on his more natural blue. His meaning was clear. *Stop staring and approach. I'll not be curt with you, but at least make yourself known to me. Sit. If you are still while I play, I'll answer your questions when I am through.*

Now Biborka flushed a True Pink. Staring was considered rude, even by The Chroma. She did as she was asked and sat down next to the Blue. *Apologies,* Biborka glowed.

The Blue barely acknowledged her apology. Instead, he turned back towards his game and lifted a pile of markers from his stack. He slid them in front of her, waving at the table with the back of his hand dismissively. Apparently, she was to join him in his game.

Biborka inclined her neck as she peered down at the board. There were colored numbers all along its surface. Reds and Blacks, alternating between the two colors as each number grew. As she watched, the Blue carefully placed his markers on top of some of the numbers. His reasoning seemed haphazard to Biborka. Black eleven, Red twenty-three, Black twenty-eight and twenty-nine. There was no discernible pattern to it she could note.

The Blue elbowed Biborka as he stared at the board. She understood she needed to place her markers as well. Carefully, Biborka chose numbers that were different from the Blue's. Some of the other players placed their markers atop his, but that seemed disrespectful to her. And she desired some symmetry. Red one, three, five, seven, and nine, each with two of her chips instead of selecting only one.

The human had already spun the wheel. After a moment, he waved his arm across the table. The betters all fell back, almost imperceptibly, in their seats, waiting and watching. The ball dropped. With a flourish, the human's maw opened, declaring something as he placed a clear token directly down on the board. It was a red square where two of her chips rested, wedging them between the board and the token. The Blue quickly allowed his annoyed orange cheeks to create a look of pleased deep violet. He had seen her correct guess. He seemed even more pleased as the human slid a large cache of markers towards her. A spike of violet ran through her as well. She could see now why the humans enjoyed this game.

Time blurred. Biborka truly couldn't say how long she sat at the table. Her stack of chips depleted itself to almost none twice. On both occasions, a miraculous win kept her in the game. She had determined that each time the ball rolled on her number, she received thirty-five chips for each one she had risked. It was enough to sustain another roll and a half. On her second near depletion, The Blue slid her just enough chips to sustain a second spin of the wheel.

At first Biborka did not see what The Blue did at the table. She was too fascinated by her own markers and how they might survive the spin. As she began to get comfortable with the game, she started to watch him as well as some of the other players. Most were stone-faced as they played. Some almost appeared bored, not even watching where the ball dropped, preferring to keep their eyes on the room or the table.

Studying The Blue from the side of her eye, never actually turning her head, he appeared far more intent than the other players. He leaned in to every spin, both elbows on the table, eyes following every little motion the spinner made as well as each leap the ball made upon the wheel. Biborka adopted his posture and mimicked him with every toss of the orb. Posed like a gargoyle atop a building, only her eyes moved as Biborka watch the ball spring from number to number. It was an entrancing sight.

Remarkably, The Blue's stack grew. He lost upon occasion, but it was infrequent. She noted, however, that his chips covered far more of the board than hers did. In fact, she assumed that he set down at least twice as many markers. In some cases, he played multiple chips on one square or buffered those squares at their corners. When the spinner found The Blue's chips on the board, his return was typically larger than Biborka's. She didn't mind though. It was enjoyable to simply play.

Biborka couldn't help but notice that The Blue would turn at odd times, looking out into the hustle of the establishment. After the third or fourth such distraction, she began to look in the direction of his gaze. Biborka began to understand that it had something to do with one blur of activity or another. How did he know these little events were occurring without having first seen them? Was this the "hearing" sensation he had implanted into his cranium? Was there really something to the awkward devices jammed into the sides of his head? She resolved to ask him when she was allowed to ask her questions. In the meantime, she continued to note the occasions and their apparent causes. They ran the gamut from a confrontation between two humans to one of the creatures celebrating after a win of some kind. The Blue grimaced at the first and smiled lightly at the second. She found his grin infectious and followed his lead in this too.

Abruptly, a new human dressed identically to the spinner arrived next to him before he could spin the orb. This one appeared to be female, a long tress trussed behind her head in some kind of tail. She mouthed something to her companion and he turned towards the table, making a slight bowing motion. Then the spinner turned and left, apparently resigning his station to the female. That appeared to be enough for The Blue. He made a motion towards his stack of markers in front of him before pushing them to the replacement spinner. She received the chips and counted them twice. Then she returned a smaller stack of numbered chips to The Blue as he stood.

Biborka looked at The Blue. A light orange of confusion puffed on her cheeks as she cocked her head at him. He motioned for her to do as he did. *Now is the time to collect your answers,* he flared back at her with a singular puff and a blur of color. It dawned on her then that The Blue was done with this game. She pushed her smaller stack to the spinner and also received a smaller, numbered stack in return. Then she stood and followed The Blue back out into the desert night.

*　　　*　　　*

Id had been Orange for far too long. Id knew because Blue and Yellow **_flared_** their concern at Id at every turn. Id could feel their eyes watching, waiting. *When?* they continued to ask each other, puffing and slinging hues without regard to who might view them. Often they were slung at a tone that made Id clamp Id's eyelids together until it stopped. It had become a daily, if not hourly event.

They weren't just Green and Yellow anymore, but Id still thought of them that way. Id had come to understand they were Id's precursors, Id's progenitors. Parents is the concept they taught Id. And they were concerned for Id. Or possibly they were concerned with the way the others of their group treated them. The looks they were given, the subtle puffs and flares the other Colors gave them when they saw Id. Or gave to each other behind their backs. Id saw the slings and arrows.

Id knew why the adults were concerned, but Id didn't care. Id would change when Id was prepared to change. And for now, Id be Orange.

*   *   *

At first Biborka thought she would have to slow her pace to keep time with The Blue, but she quickly found herself moving quite swiftly. Although she had little doubt she could best his pace, Biborka had hoped they could have ambled at a more leisurely gait if for no other reason than she could have better kept track of where they were headed. She sent out a flame of annoyance to which he responded not at all.

Biborka's eyes pleaded for The Blue to tell her anything at all, but he was resolute. He allowed only one dash of color. *When we arrive, you shall see.* Biborka paused, planting both feet down hard. The Blue didn't seem to notice. If anything his pace quickened. She stamped one foot on the ground in frustration, to no avail. Her entire visage became a nuclear orange-red and she stamped her foot again. If The Blue's implants worked as alleged and sent forth a force he could sense, then he couldn't have missed the slap of her shoe upon the ground. Still, The Blue's only reaction was to proceed. Biborka's orange flare turned a crimson worry and she sprinted to catch the elder before he became lost in the Vegas crowd outside.

They walked for a significant part of the hour without any further communication. Biborka kept a running list of turns in her head, seeking landmarks as best she could. Artificial lights, neon in particular, seemed to dominate the stroll. Until they didn't. One or two quick turns and Biborka found herself in a dingy, less-populated portion of the city. It was darker here. Here there were no tourists, their skin red from too much time in an unaccustomed sun or hats and jerseys proclaiming their allegiance to cities other than this one. Biborka felt her heart beat a dash harder. This was underground Vegas. Unseen Vegas. Only the true denizens of the city walked these streets.

The Blue stopped and faced a storefront. *Here,* he puffed. The glass was tinted heavily, although she could make out some moving forms and illuminations on the other side of the panes. A heavy wooden door rested below a sign flaking paint that proclaimed the establishment to be named Aurials. An exceptionally large red Chroma rested against the frame. He bared his broken teeth at her and Biborka felt herself reflexively retract her neck until she realized he wasn't looking at her, but rather The Blue. The realization made her no less concerned though.

The Red's eyes darted towards Biborka and then back to The Blue. *Too young, even for me,* Red sneered, holding a puff in his cheeks and scrunching his nose. The gesture was accompanied by a sickening mustard coloring.

The Blue opened his maw, spitting fluid as he addressed The Red. It was then that Biborka saw The Red was also implanted, however, he only had a single device attached to the right side of his head. His module was smaller than The

Blue's and looked as if it had been broken and reattached at least once. Likely, it had. This Red Chroma was dangerous. Biborka wished she knew what The Blue had said, especially as she watched The Red silently roar and spit back.

Horrified, yet fascinated, Biborka watched the pair jaw at each other. The Blue pointed at the establishment and at his own chest dominantly. Then he jerked his thumb at Biborka before waving the back of his hand towards The Red. His movements allowed her to fill into pieces of the conversation she was missing.

The Red pointed back at The Blue once and twice at her. His anger was apparent in more than his coloring. It was impossible to miss how it danced across his face. Conversely, The Blue seemed to have cooled to match his coloring. Finally, he made a grand sweeping gesture even she understood, despite not experiencing the words he uttered. With a final snarl of his teeth, The Red stepped to the side begrudgingly and jerked his head in the direction of the door. *Careful Izmal. Make sure the child knows the rules.*

Biborka bared her teeth at The Red, her nuclear coloring returning. Before she could object to the characterization further, The Blue put a hand on her back and pushed her towards the door. Reflexively, she turned the knob and stepped inside.

Surprisingly, the interior of Aurials was brightly lit. In addition to a comfortable coloring of stained woods and leather seating, the establishment smelled of brazed floosh and peppery grash. Like when Gromdasha cooked for

The Chroma at Drakashvlh. Biborka's stomach suddenly reminded her she hadn't eaten in quite a while.

Stepping lightly around Biborka as her senses took in everything they could, The Blue ambled towards a corner table. He waved an acknowledgment at a human woman whose hair was streaked with several streams of white through a black flow. She crossed her arms as she stood behind the bar, glaring daggers back at him. The Blue didn't seem to notice her stony gaze, but Biborka saw it clearly. Cautiously, Biborka followed him to the corner and started to set herself down across from where he sat with his back towards the wall.

No, The Blue puffed. *Here.* He pushed a seat next to him out, allowing her to put her back to the other corner wall and survey the scene. She felt like an unwelcome stranger in one of the movies the humans called Westerns. For a brief moment, the fantasy was appealing. At least until she looked around and saw her surroundings were nothing like being in such a movie.

For starters, there were no cowboy hats, pistols, or raucous patrons. In fact, there were few patrons at all. Those that were present seemed to keep to themselves or in very small, subdued groups. Not more than fifteen or twenty beings were present in what was an almost cavernous space. Perhaps it was still too early for business. She had heard that festivities in the city often didn't begin until quite late.

What was striking, however, was the co-mingling of Chroma and Human. There seemed to be an almost even split between the two species. Biborka had never seen this many of both groups in such close, and obviously friendly, proximity to each other at one time. It was fascinating, especially since she had always been warned humans didn't often like her kind. *Invaders, they call us*, her parents had puffed at her on numerous occasions. Or worse. *Earless. Pufferfish. Rainbows.* Yet here both groups seemed to have achieved some form of harmony.

The Blue flexed his jaw at the woman behind the bar. She spat something back at him, but made her way over to their table nonetheless. Instead of attending to The Blue, the human turned a pitying gaze at Biborka. She made several quick gestures with her hands at Biborka. Not knowing what else to do, Biborka's skin flared a questioning light blue. At least until she looked at The Blue. He seemed genuinely amused by her reaction, puffing mirth with his cheeks as he blared a daffodil color.

Angrily, Biborka pushed herself to her feet. *Fargut!* She wasn't going to let this human and The Blue pick on her, no matter how badly she wanted to understand this hearing thing they both had in common!

The Blue reached and lightly touched one of Biborka's hands that still rested on the table. He shook his head at her and turned an apologetic pink. *I'm not laughing at you. Just the situation. She thinks you are one of the Uninitiated and speak her primitive gesture language. Please, sit.*

Slowly, Biborka lowered herself back into the chair. The human had remained in place throughout the interaction, a puzzled expression upon her face. The Blue flapped his lips at her and the human's expression became one of understanding. He communicated something else to her and held up two digits on one hand. Then the human nodded once and turned, retreating back to the bar.

We can converse briefly before the food arrives. It actually is quite good here, probably because Gorthlg is in the kitchen tonight. Very authentic. The Blue indicated a swinging door with a circular window in the center. Through it, Biborka could see a flurry of activity on the other side. At least one Chroma could be seen through the opening.

Biborka sat back in her chair and crossed both arms over her chest, regarding The Blue with a crooked neck. Maybe this was a bad idea. Still, it was tough to ignore the smell wafting from the kitchen. She'd wait...briefly.

The Blue leaned in close to Biborka, looking both ways quickly and then turning his back slightly so his communications were obstructed from general viewing. *Call me Izmal,* The Blue signaled to her through a series of puffing cheeks, first on one side of his mouth and then the other. It was almost too quick for it to register with her.

She shrugged, holding her cocked pose. *And?* Biborka used a crimson flare. Not quite disrespectful, but certainly putting her toe upon the line. Izmal didn't appear to notice.

And this is a safe place. Ask your questions. Light blue, two patient puffs, then a return to a more dignified and natural blue. Something suiting an elder of The Chroma. In that moment, Biborka noted his plumage. Now that she sat in such close proximity to Izmal and was looking directly at his visage, she could see his scars weren't simply from aural surgery. His lost plumage hadn't expired with age either, rather it appeared to have been ripped from him. Biborka didn't allow her realization to hold her up. Finally, here was someone to enlighten her, solve the riddle that had plagued her since she began to feel doubts. Certainly these primitive creatures couldn't have a sense The Chroma didn't? How could that be possible? Just look at them. Unable to get off their own planet. And even if they could, they would undoubtedly take their war and aggressions with them. Just monkeys with ever-growing clubs.

Despite the opportunity, she didn't ask those questions. Biborka was willing to concede there may be senses The Chroma couldn't access. After all, The Zycrongzets sect claimed to feel thoughts by placing their hands atop another Chroma's head. Why not experience something called sound? Instead, Bibroka simply asked *Why?*

Biborka had uncrossed her arms and leaned in towards Izmal. She even straightened her neck. Izmal scratched his chin as he regarded the table in front of him as if the answer lay deeply embedded in the grain of the wood. His brow furrowed. When Izmal looked up at her, he flapped his lips several times. Suddenly a smile appeared on his face and a sheepish red-pink colored his face. *My apologies, sometimes I forget. I suppose, because I wanted more.*

*   *   *

Id had reached the dreaded thirty-seventh cycle. Thirty-seven cycles on Chroma. Here Id had revolved around the glowing orb in the heavens a single season past eighteen times. Id understood the humans considered their young to be grown at eighteen earth cycles. It seemed as fitting a time as ever for The Molting.

Id's colony was rife with deep eggplant hued youths. And more troubling to Id was that for every female there were five men. Idiots, Id thought. Is this in response to a perceived human aggression? Does every Chroma prepare for battle? And if they do, don't they realize that females fight as well? Likely with more skill than the males.

Although a darker color did have some appeal, Id refused to believe it would be any more a deterrent for aggression. Id enjoyed a lilac or even a lavender. Violet had some appeal as well. Perhaps something in the middle. In truth, it didn't matter much to Id. But it was time to be free of orange androgyny. It was time to make a selection.

Id waited for night to fall and snuck out of the yorgt. Id always walked lightly, but that night Id paid extra attention to Id's steps. The door creaked slightly, causing Id to freeze. When no other sound reverberated within the walls, Id pushed it open a fraction more and slipped through.

Outside, the dry air had dropped in temperature. The desert can be cold during the evenings, no matter how hot the sands were during the day. Id relished the cool, light breeze as Id left small indentations in the desert with bare feet. At first, Id had no intention of wandering far, but a strong pull to wander dragged the fledgling Chroma a fair ways into the desert. There was a sense that it was simply more peaceful the farther in Id meandered.

Once Id was far enough into the desert to be assured no one else was around, yet close enough to still see the settlement, Id collapsed into the sand. Lying down and gazing at the glittering orbs in the clear sky, Id released the tension built up in Id's body. The relief was far more pleasurable than Id thought it would be. Id had been holding everything in so tightly for so long that it practically exploded outward like a doorway bursting off its hinges had it not been for Id's firm metaphysical grip.

First Id let the orange slip away, fighting internally so that the process didn't flow too quickly. Id wanted to remember this moment, another reason for changing at night all alone. The sky was deep purple, but just over the horizon there was a light. Id knew it was the city. The most beautiful colors seemed to flow from it, even at this distance. Perhaps the distance is what made it so beautiful. Id seized upon a lavender color that flowered over the metropolis. That was the one, Id thought and willed it into Id's plumage. Then slowly, with some real effort, Id allowed it to seep in deeper. Once Id's hue had been determined, there were two more decisions to make. A gender and what to call oneself.

* * *

Biborka had many more questions. Was it worth it? Did it hurt? Would Izmal do it again? She peppered him mercilessly. Izmal answered each with the patience of an Elder, even though he didn't wear the arm bangles or elaborate cloak. Not that all Elders encumbered themselves so, but it was a sure status sign amongst The Chroma. Just before the food arrived, his exasperation finally allowed itself to shine through.

So, little one whose name I do not even know, why did you follow an old Chroma to an unknown bar in a desolate section of this blinding city? Was it merely to gawk and question one at the end of his life cycle? What was left of Izmal's feathering flared a tiger orange on one puff and then cooled to a burnt hue on the next. Biborka felt the pink rising at her collar. She was saved from answering when a plate was suddenly deposited in front of her. So intent had she been on things that Biborka didn't even see their server arrive with steaming plates.

The pair ate in silence. Biborka did manage a thankful gesture in the server's direction. It didn't appear to be acknowledged, but she didn't know if that was because the gesture wasn't understood or merely ignored.

Although she tried to take her time consuming the meal, Biborka eventually gave in and devoured it. It was delicious fare, almost indistinguishable from what she would have received at home. This was authentic Chroma cooking. Once it was completed, Bibroka pushed the plate away from her. Then she delicately studied Izmal as he ate. He was far slower to consume his victuals. And he continued to pointedly ignore her.

It is Biborka. She puffed delicately so as no one else would pick up on the movements and read them. Izmal merely paused before looking back down at the food he was consuming and nodded once. Then Izmal resumed his ever so deliberate ingestion.

The waitress returned only once and was quickly waved away by a flick of Izmal's wrist and two quick flaps of his jaw. Apparently that was the signal for her to stay away. After what felt like all of eternity, Izmal pushed his plate away and leaned back in his chair. Biborka had long since been done with her meal and had been trying mostly unsuccessfully to stop the unconscious shaking of her right leg and tapping of her left thumb on the table. Izmal didn't glare at her, but his coloring showed a mild annoyance. Finally Biborka could contain her questions no longer.

Why do you hide here? Biboka's plumes flared a pure white, marking that it had been a question without malice. No sooner had she asked than she colored an embarrassed pink. That might not have been a polite question, she realized, even if her plumage showed her to be earnest.

Izmal shrugged. *Where else is there to go?* He smiled, but his feathering gave him away. It wasn't the dirty white of surrender, but rather a rueful and acerbic rose. He quickly corrected his coloring, possibly due to Biborka's corresponding furrowing of her brow more in a pitying gesture than confusion, but it was too late. Biborka held her stare.

Because, but for my curiosity, I become a pariah in two worlds rather than a curiosity in one and an enemy in the other. Izmal puffed and flared. *Hybrids are not liked in either community.*

So you are an outcast? Biborka surmised, a sky blue of understanding dawning upon her plumage.

Biborka was primed to ask another question, but Izmal's head suddenly jerked in the direction of the doorway. When she followed his eyes, she could see some kind of scuffle had broken out. Or perhaps assault. Surprise colored her features as Biborka realized that the Red watching the doorway had crashed to the ground, his body's black ichor dripping from his forehead and spattering the floor. The entrance was wide open and a hoard of humans had bullied their way inside.

*　　　*　　　*

Id admitted to Id's self that the gender hadn't been a difficult decision. Thought had been put into it, but in truth the decision was easy and obvious. The male of the species was at best fumbling and at worst brutish or even bellicose. They tended not to live as long as their counterparts. A need to flash their plumage and be seen ended in many untimely deaths. The need for attention alone made Id balk.

Of course, Id wasn't **required** to make a decision. Their were those of Id's race that lived a long and health life perfectly genderless or in some cases, multigendered. Id's species even had those that transitioned from one gender to the other, in rare cases more than once. But Id wasn't so young and naive not to see how they were treated. There were whispered stories of those who had been forced to conform to a gender against their will by Elders. The thought of losing that choice sickened Id.

It was said one became more *resolute* in one's opinions and feeling the longer one remained in a gender. Better to pick one that suited Id. Id supposed that a change could always be made if desired.

Id wasn't concerned about being an outcast. Besides the obvious benefits of femininity, there was a deeper reason Id gravitated towards the selected gender. Id's race had a ratio of roughly four males to every female, even after taking into consideration the higher death rate. Id wasn't making the decision in an effort to be unique, but rather to ensure the species continued survival on this backward planet. It was true that more males willing to battle the humans should the need arise would be useful, but not nearly as useful as creating more Chroma. There was a magic in that decision to create rather than destroy.

But a name...a name would prove more challenging...

*   *   *

Biborka! Girl...Biborka, quickly now! Izmal was fluttering his feathers so quickly they blurred. A rush of colors accompanied the haze.

She was frozen. It wasn't that she didn't want to move, she simply couldn't. Her eyes were wide open, taking in the picture of horror in front of her, and appendages simply refused to comply with the commands Biborka was sending them. Perhaps worst of all, the mob of incensed humans seemed to have focused on her.

In her peripherals, Izmal's colors flitted like a panicked bird or an irate wasp's wings. Biborka felt him clutch her arm underneath her pit, hauling her up. Vaguely she noted that he was stronger than he appeared. Although standing, she remained motionless, fixated still on the rush of the crowd. Their mouths were open, presumably blaring whatever garish noise these creatures were alleged to make from their holes.

Izmal shook her to no avail. Finally he grabbed her chin and jerked it so that her eyes aligned with his. *Run, or we die!* Izmal declared in a crimson so dark it broke the spell. She had never seen such a tint before, although it wasn't the wonder of the hue that shattered the magic, but rather the pure depravity of the color and intensity that shone from his feathers. Biborka had seen terms that passed for curses in her language, but nothing so shocking as that color's bloody grime awash across her companion.

And so they ran. Not towards the outer door where death lurked, but towards the wall at their back. Izmal pulled and she complied. Biborka was so panicked, it took her an extra moment to realize they were headed toward an insurmountable object. There could be no purchase along this wall, it was solid stone. She flashed an alarmed scarlett followed by the vivid red of panic at Izmal. Still he pulled her.

Just as they were about to bound headlong into solid rock, Izmal arm swiped against the wall. It moved, like drapes in front of an open window or the curtain of a stage. Biborka wished she had more than a moment to take it in before she crashed through the opening hidden by the cloth concealment. It truly was an ingenious deception. She had sat next to it all through her dinner and hadn't noticed so much as a seam. Whoever had designed it had been a true craftsman. This escape tunnel had been planned for some time. Clearly the owners had anticipated such an attack could occur.

They dashed through the dark corridor at a breakneck pace. Biborka stumbled once, but caught herself before falling. She kept her eye squarely on Izmal's back, navigated exactly like he did - ducking when he ducked, twisting when the passage was narrow, and even crawling on her hands and knees. The entire time, the hairs on the back of her neck raised themselves on full alert. She couldn't tell if anyone followed them, but a sixth sense insisted others, either friend or foe, were fast on their heels.

Izmal stopped short and Biborka narrowly avoided crashing into his back. They had come to a dead end, nothing was infront of them except a gritty concrete wall. Biborka was breathing so hard that she could almost feel the air flee her chest like a jet blasting away from the runway. Her lungs flared as if they were the plane's afterburner. Feathers flittered angrily, raging in reds and oranges that could not be seen in the dark of the escapeway. Biborka didn't know if Izmal could see her anger mixed with fright and frustration, but if he could, it was quickly soothed.

A hand grasped Birborka's tight. In surprise, she attempted to pull it away. Izmal's grip was shockingly strong and he held her despite the quick reactive jerk. With his other hand Izmal felt along the wall. In the darkness, she could just make out how his fingers found a crease in the blockwork. He pulled and the wall slid open the slightest amount. It was just enough for them to slide through one at a time. Izmal went first, gently holding her hand as he guided her through the opening. As soon as they were both through, Izmal released his grip and the wall suddenly closed again.

Biborka found herself in an all encompassing darkness. Her heart thumped against her chest and she reached up to lay a hand across it as if that would still it's hammering. Instead, she could only feel it thrash inside her harder. Biborka inhaled hard. Cut off in the darkness from a sense she depended on so heavily, all she could feel was sheer terror. She flung her hands out in front of her, but felt nothing. Nothing to the sides either. Not knowing what else to do, Biborka leaned against the wall and sank down along it until she was in a squatting position. Then she put her hands over her face and wept.

*   *   *

There was something about the deep purple hues of the night that resonated with Id in this seemingly desolate wasteland. Here in the night all wasn't a pitch impenetrable darkness, rather it was a gentle blanket enveloping Id as if wrapped in a mother's arms. Even the shadows moved around Id more like dancers than unknown terrors of a youth's imagination. Id felt comfortable here.

Id would keep this moment somehow in Id's Naming. The deep hues in the night sky, like an impressionist canvas with its violets and dark blues and royal purples, would remain with Id in Id's to be assumed Name. Id drank the night, ate the colors of the sky, and smelled the dry air. Id had a name to honor this night and these colors. The transformation could begin.

Lying face upwards to the heavens, arms and legs splayed outwards on the ground, Id's eyelids calmly closed. Id didn't need any instruction. Every Chroma had the instinct to Become locked within. One simply had to surrender to it. And so Id did exactly that. Surrender.

Id could feel plumage feathering, growing. If one could ever *feel* a color, The Becoming would be that moment. Id knew Id's plumage was slowly coloring itself a light purple. It would begin at the roots and push outward. Similarly, Id's anatomy pushed out in some areas and grew inward in others.

It wasn't painful per se. Rather the tingle of Becoming was almost pleasurable at times, like scratching an itch just a bit too much and drawing blood. It felt good to satiate the urge, alleviating the urgent need and then going past pleasure to pain and finally mixing the two together, knowing all the while that it was important to stop but not wanting to because the sensation was so powerfully addictive.

Itch after itch was scratched, over and over again in waves all across Id's body. Or, Id supposed, her body. There was no denying after what felt like hours but was likely mere minutes, Id was now a female. Eyes still closed, she explored her body, poking gently at new parts and running her fingers along her feathers. The plumage felt no different, but she knew its color would be a drastic change.

Once the cursory inspection had been completed, she sighed and opened her eyes. Deep purples still swirled over her. Purple. Her name would have to involve the color. It would be a fitting homage to the night that wrapped around her.

There had been a book written by a Hungarian woman. She didn't remember the author's name, but recalled her hero. The protagonist had fought a good fight, but nevertheless she succumbed to a martyr's demise. She would take that name, both for its meaning and a desire to display a similar nobility should her time arise.

And so Biborka rose and made her way towards the shining lights of the city. There was so much she wanted to learn.

*   *   *

A blinding streak of white destroyed the darkness. Or so it seemed. In truth it was the merest flicker of illumination, but it took Biborka by surprise and required processing. Once the initial blaze had passed, she realized that Izmal held a small lighter in his hand. He shielded it with the other so as to keep its illumination low. The flame did not allow for her to see the entirety of the room, leaving long darknesses in the distance, but it did let her see Izmal lit up in the sickly yellow reflected by the flame and the jaundiced concern of his chroma.

Now heed me.

His concern, or possibly fear, only deepened his coloring. Biborka was too paralyzed by her own fear to respond. Instead she leaned in towards him to assure she caught every gesture, every flash of color he conveyed, no matter how briefly. She nodded simply.

Good. You want to know why. Why I would deface myself so, become a pariah no matter where I go. That is why you sought me out.

Izmal waited, his feathers now still, taking on a grayish neutral color. She looked back at him, studying his face, his eyes. Izmal looked tired, defeated. Maybe the gray of his coloring was less patience and more surrender. What was he doing? Biborka attempted to keep her own coloring a simple tan to show she was attentive, but it was difficult to keep a flash of confusion from her feathers.

Because there is more. And we are creatures who adapt. Who make ourselves. We are not made to remain static, no matter what dogma The Chroma peddle about our place in things. And we are not simply what these small humans would have us be, even if it was their orb first. They aren't all bad, but they are limited.

Izmal leaned in slightly and Biborka could almost feel his emphasis in her chest as his plumage flared to life in a cacophony of colors, whirling like a dervish along his whole being.

So go. Explore. Be fluid. Be what you envision. And if you wish to experience more than our biology, then do so.

And then the light was gone. *Fargut!* Biborka felt her chest spike adrenaline the moment she was enveloped. And suddenly there was a hand on hers. It grasped her tightly for the merest moment, before letting up and pressing something into it. The object was hot and stung her palm as Izmal pressed what Biborka realized was the lighter.

Birborka was confused, but not for more than a moment. Izmal pushed her away and she stumbled to her feet as the door to their hiding place slid open, revealing ugly faces bifurcated by the light. How did he know they were there? Was Izmal's acquired sense responsible for his awareness?

Biborka had little time to dwell on the thought. She continued to stumble, now backwards into the darkness as arms grasped Izmal, dragging him into the light of their pursuers' devices. His feathers, which had taken on the darkest of colors, flared one final message in the most pure gold Biborka had ever encountered.

Go!

Tears streaming down her face, Biborka fled into the darkness. She flicked the flint of the lighter only once she had slipped to the edges of the shadows and was certain the humans were more interested in Izmal than her.

Biborka found a narrow hallway and hurriedly followed it, the tips of her fingers scraping along the wall as she went. After an eternity, she found a door. Cautiously, she opened it and emerged into the light of the day.

*　　*　　*

She wandered aimlessly. Or perhaps it would be more accurate to describe her meanderings as without anything but the basest of instincts. Biborka obeyed crosswalks and the flashing lights that told when it was safe to tread upon them, but little else. And when she was too tired to continue, she flopped against a well and slid down it. She remained in that pose until the darkness descended and attempted to envelop the city. It was quickly beaten back by the blaring dissonance of the settlement's neon lighting. And yet, the shadows somehow continued to surround Biborka.

A single tear slipped down her cheek. Biborka refused to touch it and let it dry itself where it fell. Then she closed both eyes and slipped into Phantasos' realm.

*   *   *

Biborka woke to the sensation of someone kicking her legs. Or so it felt. Slowly regaining consciousness, she saw that a human had tripped over her. He lay face down on the sidewalk. His chest moved up and down, so she knew he was alive. There was a splash of blood on the pavement next to his head. And what looked like a tooth. She could smell a mixture of sweat and alcohol upon him despite what looked like finely tailored clothing. When she saw the rusty ichor, she recoiled and her legs instinctively pushed her upright and away from the fallen body.

Her lip curled upwards as Biborka looked at this pathetic creature lying in front of her. Was *this thing* another who would like to see her and those like her harmed? Thrown from the planet back into the cold emptiness from which they arrived? She didn't remember what the humans who violently dragged Izmal off looked like, there were too many of them and it had been too dark. In truth, she remembered nothing but the feeling of panic. It had since receded to loathing and disappointment in herself. She had abandoned Izmal. He was probably dead.

Anger blossomed within her. Unable to hold herself back, Biborka kicked the human lying in front of her. Hard. Her foot hit a squishy area and sank in. The body convulsed. Disgusted in herself, she stepped back and looked down at her appendage. It was free of blood, so she couldn't have hurt him any more than the fall had already.

She should leave. Go back home and pretend this *adventure* had never happened. She could declare her name to the Chroma. Everyone, most of all her parents, would be relieved. Then she could live the life of a dutiful citizen. Forget anything ever happened in this gaudy city of human folly.

Biborka sidestepped the prone body. She looked down at it one last time as she passed. Under where the human's head lay was a blue feather. It could have been from anything. A bird. A costume. Certainly not something from the Chroma. Certainly not...

Her shoulders slumped. Was this a sign or her subconscious looking for an excuse not to walk away. She could still feel her fear and rage, but another emotion wormed away in her gut. Maybe it was guilt, although for exactly which of the day's transgressions she was uncertain. Action or inaction, both assaulted her sense of justice. In the end, action won out.

Shaking the human man's shoulders, Biborka flared a violent red. *Awake!* She emoted towards the sickly thing. It convulsed, possibly from her kick to its ribs. She shook it again with no additional result. Finally, Biborka flipped it onto his back to get a better look. The blue feather remained glued to his forehead by the slowly congealing blood on his face. It was a gruesome scene. Bruises decorated the man's face and a jagged cut bled. She couldn't tell if the fall to the sidewalk had caused it or if the injury predated the man's tumble. Perhaps more than alcohol was involved here.

The man gasped suddenly for breath. To Biborka, he looked like a fish struggling for water. The eye not obstructed by the feather opened and it slowly focused on her as she loomed over the man. A mild surprise registered on the human's face before he tightly shut both orbs and raised one appendage to delicately pick the feather off of his visage. Instead of casting it away, however, he slowly opened his eyes and examined the blood-encrusted object. Then he gently put it into a front pocket and regarded her.

The man's mouth opened and closed several times. Biborka realized that he was attempting to communicate with her. She feathered back at him a confused light orange. He squinted at her flurry as if he were trying to read very small lettering. Then he nodded and pulled something out of his pocket.

At first, Biborka was confused by the object. It was small and furry and brightly multicolored. In fact, it seemed to be a cloth with all the colors. The man, still lying on his back, whirled the cloth around so that it was nothing but a blur of red. Then he stopped, flipped the cloth to an orange setting, and whirled it again. He repeated this red then orange combo twice before it dawned on Biborka that he was trying to communicate with her.

A flash of lightning yellow exploded through Biborka's feathers. The man was asking her for help. He was imploring her to pick him up like a child asks a parent using the few limited colors and patterns it understands. Without thinking, Biborka reached down and grasped the man's hand. With some effort and two tries, she was able to get him to his feet. His cloth whirled a thank you before he tucked it back into his pocket and began to stagger away. Within three steps, he fell to one knee.

Biborka rushed over to him before the man could fall completely over onto the ground again. She ducked to one knee and stabilized him. Then she put an arm around his back and together they pushed upwards. Finally they began walking together shoulder to shoulder very deliberately along the sidewalk.

Humans moved out of their way or pretended not to notice the odd pair teeter along. The human raised a hand on occasion and pointed in a direction. Left. Right. Right. They didn't walk very far, but they did walk for some time. Eventually, they arrived at a small office. The man's face was on the door smiling.

It proclaimed he was a doctor, specializing in reconstruction, whatever that was. The door was locked when she grasped the handle.

Biborka felt a tap on her back as the man slid away from her. She dropped her arm and let him lean against the wall. Slowly, he fished through his pockets and recovered a small key. Instead of trying it himself, he handed it to her. She felt the bolt move and pulled the door open. Then Biborka put her arm back around the man to help him enter the darkened office.

He collapsed into a chair in the waiting room and she found the light. It was small, only three chairs and a little cube for a receptionist. Apparently, the man wasn't particularly successful at reconstruction. He pointed to the receptionist's desk and mimed a sliding motion. Biborka understood and opened the top drawer revealing a single object. In it was a much larger and complex version of the man's colored cloth. She handed it to him, a curious color on her plumage.

Thank you for your assistance. I'm lucky a Woman of the Chroma came along. I fear my own people would have let me die in the street.

The larger cloth made understanding him much easier. Biborka still had to watch closely, but it was amazing how well he communicated in her language. It was as if he was a youth, learning their ways and spreading his wings. He could almost pass for a Purple at times.

Biborka couldn't help herself, her questions spewed from her completely unbidden. Like a child herself, she asked many disparate things all at once.

How can you speak to me? How did you get this device? You humans are practically blind, yet you use our chroma like one raised amongst us. Who taught you?

The man smiled, perhaps not understanding everything she blurred at him in her rainbow haste. He did seem to get the gist of it.

My patients taught me. It was a simple flourish. Then he cocked his head away from her, one of his lobes now in full view. The gesture revealed a small implanted device inserted within one of the crevesses. Another turn of his head revealed a similar contraption on the other side. The cloth flashed in his hands. *In some ways, I am just like you. Or, rather, those of the Chroma who also long to gather the color that is not a color.*

It was like a shot to her heart. There were humans who needed technological aids to communicate with their own kind? Didn't they all have some secret invisible language the Chroma couldn't access without implants? Unbidden, Biborka sat in one of the chairs in the lobby. She had never considered there were humans like her. They were such strange creatures.

Are you well? The doctor's back had straightened and he had pushed himself halfway out of his seat. Biborka waved at him and he collapsed back down. He seemed relieved.

It. It is alot to comprehend. A simple gray. Something neutral to dissuade his alarm. Inside though, Biborka was roiling. Why didn't someone tell The Chroma? Did they already know there were humans like them? And what about the humans? Did they know as well? Someone needed to tell them.

Thoughts of Izmal's last moments before he sacrificed himself for her raged in her breast. She could feel a red wash through her feathering and stopped it before she could alarm her companion. Surely Izmal would have told them, wouldn't he? Were The Chroma as much at fault for their isolation as the humans? Biborka closed her eyes and inhaled sharply. She held them shut tight for a long moment. Then she snapped them open and asked the question that she finally realized she had wanted to ask since she left the dessert.

Your device. How does one get something like that? Biborka pointed to where the little metal pieces protruded from the man's ears.

I'm a doctor. I implant them. He pointed towards a sign at the desk that read Dr. Ambrose. Beneath it was a smiling photo of the man with a patient. It was faded, making Biborka feel as if it had been taken in better times. A look at the good doctor's present maligned visage confirmed it.

What happened? Her query was genuine. Dr. Ambrose looked much better in his photo than in his current state. It wasn't simply his injuries. He now looked worn, a tire tread that needed to be replaced or a wall in desperate need of another coat of paint to fight the desert sun's rays. This man might have once had a thriving practice. Now she would be surprised if he saw two patients a day. Or more correctly, if two patients a day would trust him with their health.

He shrugged. Then with a wince, Ambrose pulled himself up so that he could peer into her eyes. A sad smile replaced the obvious pain as he flashed the color wheel cloth.

Your people happened. And I helped them. It did not endear me to my own kind. The smile went away and Ambrose pushed himself upright. He wobbled, but remained vertical. *I guess they didn't feel as similar to you as I did.*

One foot in front of the other and at a plodding pace, Ambrose made his way to a doorway. The other side revealed a hallway with three more doors. One was open, obviously where a patient would await his arrival for diagnosis. The exam table had run out of its standard paper covering, underneath was a cracking faux leather that had clearly been worn away by patient usage. Supplies appeared limited, but an old magazine did sit next to the examination table on a plain wooden table.

Biborka followed Ambrose as he staggered in through one of the closed doors and slumped into a comfortable chair in a barren office. He seemed like he might lose consciousness so she trailed him into his sanctum. The wall had several framed diplomas, but were otherwise barren. When she looked just a bit closer, Biborka saw a number of discolorations on the wall, almost like a variety of other awards or personal items of varying size had been pinned there and kept the sunlight from the office's one window from bleaching those spots. Now nothing prevented the sun's rays as it attacked those holes.

Her assessment of the meager office complete, Biborka looked back towards Ambrose. He had closed his eyes and his chest was moving up and down at a measured pace. She shook his shoulder lightly and he opened one eye.

You hit your head. Shouldn't you remain awake?

Ambrose made a face, but nodded in agreement. He pulled himself a bit higher in his seat and leaned forward. Biborka could see it was a struggle for him. She dragged a stool from the other room into his office and sat opposite Ambrose. She would simply have to keep an eye on him a bit longer.

So, tell me about the device in your ear. Her question was the very color of curiosity. Ambrose smiled and snatched at his cloth to respond. Some vigor seemed to come back to him as Ambrose manipulated the cloth. Slowly at first, but as he went on, a passion for his work was revealed.

They allow me to...understand the waves of sound. To communicate with others.

Biborka rolled her eyes before flashing them at Ambrose impatiently. She knew that already. He smiled at her like a parent humoring a child.

I...manipulated others like them. It took a lot of work, but eventually I created ones that suited your kind.

Biborka was confused. Why would he do that? Did someone in the Chroma ask him to make them?

No. Ambrose smiled sadly. *I did it at first because it seemed interesting. The opportunity to work on alien physiology was a challenge. Then it became an obsession. My human patients were confused, many left because they didn't trust your kind. The rest left when the bigots threatened me and anyone who showed up here. I had to close.*

A heat rose up within Biborka. She could feel herself getting angry. Were humans really so pathetic? She was certain her feathering was a deep red as she blasted a query at him.

So you no longer help Chroma who wish to receive these implants?

He shook his head and sank back into the chair. Ambrose cocked his head, regarding her clinically. He didn't make any other response for a long second. Biborka wondered if her anger might have violated some kind of ethic she didn't understand. Finally she understood why he was studying her.

I still help some. Not here. And not during the day. You helped me and I will help you if you wish.

Ambrose gestured to the devices on his head. At first she didn't realize what he was offering. When she had left the safety of the Chroma, this was certainly not where she thought she would end up. In fact, she had had a deep suspicion that she would have been back within the safety of home within mere hours. She knew this was something life changing. Something she should really give much thought to before accepting or denying Ambrose's offer. She **knew** that, yet...

Yes. Yes, I would like that.

Ambrose nodded, his mouth opening and closing quickly. Although she did not understand him, Biborka felt a thrill rush through her body. Soon, she would.

*   *   *

They waited in Ambrose's office for several hours. Biborka could feel her stomach burn with the need for sustenance. Just when she didn't think she could handle it much longer, Ambrose stood up and signaled to her that it was time to leave. She immediately suppressed the urge to eat and bolted upright to follow him. The excitement quickly outweighed her hunger.

Ambrose went first, looking both ways outside the door before he opened it fully so she could exit. It was dark out, but not entirely night. Between the waning glow of the sun and the bright lights of the city, nighttime was only a basic observance. Then he promptly locked it behind them.

During their wait, Ambrose had washed the blood from his face. No one was likely to stop them based on his appearance. He has also given her an article of clothing with a hood and advised Biborka to use it. Although a lone female of the Chroma might only arouse a slight suspicion, one walking with a human would certainly raise some eyebrows. Biborka's sense of fairness fought with her internally, but ultimately she decided to wear the disguise. It was simply easier.

The streets were empty, but to Biborka they had a looming feeling of sinister expectation. She allowed herself many glances from under her hood to look at the doorways and windows of each building they passed. It felt to her that shadows peered out from each alley and aperture, but nothing emerged to impede them. Her pace quickened until she felt a hand close itself over her shoulder. Biborka started before remembering that Ambrose was walking with her. He appeared out of sorts.

Slowly. It still hurts to walk.

Biborka chastised herself inwardly. No matter how foreboding this city now felt nor how strong her desire to sprint away from it might be, she wouldn't feel right leaving Ambrose to fend for himself, even if he appeared far better in just these last few hours. And in any case, how would she know where to go?

With great effort, Biborka slowed her pace. She looped an arm around Ambrose in order to assure she matched his steps. His appendage was reassuring and the dull terror receeded. Eventually, they arrived.

Biborka expected some great secret underground lab or possibly even a coven of similarly hooded individuals armed with weaponry and peering out windows suspiciously. At the very least, she had envisioned a secret knock of some kind. None of these things came to pass. Instead they stood before yet another plain office building. Ambrose waved a card in front of the door and it opened automatically.

They passed a bored security guard. A nameplate that declared "Harold" was on duty. The term was a stretch as the man was sleeping. Or at least had his eyes closed as he reclined in a chair at the desk. He never once even looked up.

After passing through two sterile white hallways, Ambrose stopped at a plain wooden door. He waved his pass for a second time. Again the door opened. Inside it was dark, but when Ambrose flipped on the switch, the lab suddenly came brilliantly into focus. The room, like the hallways, was starkly white in appearance. Biborka's eyes squinted as she attempted to bring it all to bear. There were two reclining seats, presumably for the patients to be operated upon.

Various medical equipment hovered near the seating. A sink, cleaning materials and several cabinets were the only other things that resided there.

Ambrose held out his arm towards one of the recliner seats. He didn't watch to see if she sat. Instead he began to rifle through one of the cabinets. Not knowing exactly what Ambrose was looking for or how she might assist him, Biborka opted to accept his offer and lay down on the chair. It wasn't overly comfortable, but that didn't matter much to Biborka. She hadn't realized how exhausted she was until she relaxed. Her lids were too heavy to resist and she slipped into slumber.

*   *   *

They gawked at her. The colors ranged from curious light blues to mildly disapproving pinks and finally red rage. None feathered approval. She didn't know why. What were they all so intent upon? What had she done?

She was encircled. A flurry of feathers flapped furiously, blocking any escape. She recognized faces melting in and out like swirling mists. Her father. Her mother. Friends, foes, relatives. Some of the faces were completely foriegn.

Izmal was there too. The devices in his head were not. He looked at her blankly, cocking his head in thought. Then he turned away. She thought she sensed his disappointment as he disappeared into the conflagration. Other faces jeered at her, but their impact had suddenly faded. None hit her as hard as Izmal.

Anger beat in her chest. Why wasn't he happy for her? Was what she had done truly so horrible? She clenched her fists then bombarded forward to chase him. How dare he!

The mist grew thicker. Unseen hands pushed, pulled, pinched, punched and slapped her. She could feel welts raise, but she didn't stop following Izmal. It wasn't hard to keep on his trail. His outline glowed, making it simple to trail him despite the mist and the darkness it brought.

Finally, Izmal stopped. He had nowhere else to go and she was almost upon him. Standing upon a ledge, his back to her, he peered downward. She reached out to grab Izmal's shoulder but was a step too slow.

Leaning forward, Izmal pitched himself over the ledge. Into the mist. Into a darkness so thick there could be nothing at the bottom but more fall.

*　　　*　　　*

Biborka woke with a start, lashing out. Her arm caught another's before she realized it was only Ambrose. His hand had shaken her shoulder lightly, but now he fell back, surprised at the force of her attack. Hands both held upward, Ambrose posed as if to surrender to her.

You slept. Dreamt. I left you alone until you appeared to be in distress.

Bibroka nodded and puffed an apology. Ambrose smiled back acceptingly. As she sat up, she realized tools and other equipment were laid out all around her. Ambrose must have spent the time preparing for whatever he was going to do to her. Biborka grimaced with determination.

I'm ready.

Are you sure? Ambrose scratched his chin and grimaced. Biborka was no expert at deciphering human emotions, but she wondered if he was more concerned than he appeared. Was that a nervous gesture or was she reading too much into it?

She nodded back at him. *Yes. No more delaying.*

Ambrose held up two small electronic devices. They appeared similar at first, but when Biborka examined them more closely, it was clear they were mismatched. Both were varying degrees of purple, although one was slightly larger than the other.

I didn't have two that matched. Ambrose showed her a small box with several similar devices in them. They ranged in color and size. She didn't see any matching pairs. Or any others with her tones. *They work. And should blend in with your feathers.*

Biborka collapsed back into the chair as Ambrose flitted around her. He checked instruments two, three times. Then he laid all of his tools out on a table near her head. Monitoring equipment was strapped across her body. Biborka could see the results on a monitor next to her. Finally, Ambrose dragged a machine with a hose attached to it. The hose ended in some kind of mask with a strap. He handed it to her and tapped his head.

You don't want to be awake for this. I promise no harm will come to you, but it will be painful. I have to bore into—

Biborka cut him off by pulling the mask over her head. Ambrose reached over and tightened the straps. Once they were secure he twisted a dial. She drew a breath sharply. What have I done? She wondered. Then... all went dark.

*   *   *

This time there were no dreams. No veiled warnings to herself. No plays upon her insecurities. No questions if she had made the proper choices. Biborka simply opened her eyes and found herself staring upon the off-white ceiling.

Unfortunately, the color made other things obvious. Speckles of bronze and rust appeared near a pond shaped stain. Somewhere, possibly from a slow leak, water was getting in. It must have been a while since Ambrose's last client or she guessed the problem would have been fixed. Or perhaps it had, but no one bothered to clean and paint.

The stain wasn't what caught her attention though. That was simply something to fix her eyes upon. The first two things Biborka noticed, in inverse order, was a throb on the sides of her head and a sensation that she could not identify. It was both pleasant and piercing. For some reason she wanted to feel more of it.

Biborka sat up and reached for the right side of her head. Where there had once been a slight divot that was covered over by skin and feathering, now rested a cool plastic shape embedded surgically into her cranium. Her eyes bulged in recognition of the device Ambrose had shown her before he knocked her out. In correspondence, her feathers flashed from red to orange to yellow and finally to an accepting midnight blue.

As she looked across from her, she saw that Ambrose sat next to her. He was regarding her impassionately and had some kind of metal fork in his hands that he was repeatedly pinging against her chair. Biborka realized she had found the source of sensation she could not identify upon waking.

Ambrose had no cloth to communicate. He made no attempt to look for it either. Rather he simply hit the fork against the table again and brought it up to her new implant. Bibroka could feel something emanate from it and down into the very core of her chest. She flinched back, one eye inadvertently squinting.

As quickly as Ambrose had brought the fork to one side of her head, he brought it across to the other. The force of the object had lessened slightly, but she still felt it. She forced herself to keep both eyes open defiantly. Ambrose nodded his head and smiled. Then his maw opened, revealing something truly terrifying.

It took Biborka a brief moment to realize what she was experiencing. Whether it was her recent drug induced rest or simply her first time experiencing the sensation, Biborka understood the surgery was successful. She smiled back at Ambrose, an enormous lopsided grin filled with all of the joy she could ever possibly communicate. A rainbow flared to life across her body, fireworks blasting in a million different directions. The vibrations of that little fork, along with the deep timbre of his voice, were the first two things she had ever heard.

"Kan yoo heer mee?" Ambrose asked. "Beeborkaw?"

Biborka only grinned, slightly smaller this time. And slowly, as deliberately as her body would allow her, Biborka began to rein in all the colors streaking through her plumage. Ambrose certainly knew the answer, he needed no translation to tell him what she felt. Had he not been through this self same elation once?

Biborka could break the silence, but she didn't have to do it now. In her time, when she was ready, she would hear her own voice. But for now, she simply wanted to take in that which was around her.

*   *   *

They were below. Down. There. That was her destination. In the sandy valley as the glowing bronze orb warily peeked over the horizon. Although still rubbing its own salt from its eyes, the sun's lethargy did not impact her in the least. She was determined. She would descend.

She paused, not from fear, but rather to savor the moment. To watch the long shadows of the dwellings shorten.To breathe in the dry air before its temperature discouraged inhalation. To watch the light flicker along her feathers as they shone in the deepest of purple. And to take in the sheer beautiful stillness below her before the bustle began. Some would call it quiet, but to one who had only just understood what silence truly was, this outpost was deafening.

And finally she stopped her progress for one more reason. She had already rehearsed her part. Over and over, it tumbled through her head and swam across her feathers. It screamed in an urgent spectrum of color that defied any that doubted it. It blared in the language of her people.

But there was one thing she still had yet to do. One medium she had yet to use to express her findings. To plead her case. To warn her people. Or even to simply indulge for herself.

For she had yet to hear her own voice. But that was about to change.

And so she descended.

Render

A novella of a fractal mind
lost through time.

By
Joshua Lee Andrew Jones

Edited by Mark C. Frankel

Render

Many had called Horus odd, but he never took it as an insult. Even when it was meant to be. With a beleaguered sigh, Lilly Harcourt referred to his rapid fire but detailed answers as odd at the job interview. He had been lost in automatic mode, a condition to which he was prone, and thought about how her name paralleled her appearance. Flowery. Yet she was very familiar. That was another inquiry for another day though.

Part of his mind was answering the interview questions as the other was speeding through the etymology of the name Lilium. Latin based but derived through Greek, Coptic, and perhaps back to an extinct language. Extinct like some lepidoptera larvae that once used the flowers as a food source.

Partitioning his mind was something he knew others could not do, so Horus tried to keep it private. The ability manifested when things got tedious. Sadly, that was most days.

In the office far taller than wide, Lilly fidgeted with the string of pearls on her tapered neck while the ceiling fan droned a hypnotic hum. As she spoke, Horus envisioned her as a white lily withering under the sun. Only when she commented on how she found the spelling of his name unusual, and not of what she deemed a proper Horace, did he break the trance and cycled his thoughts down into the moment. A hearty congratulations had confused him. Then he realized what had happened.

His degrees and accomplishment in the world of science won him the job but he did not remember much of his past. Everything from three years ago forward he recalled in perfect and pristine order. Memories from before only came like flashbulbs burning his sight. Never focused but bright and soon faded. He could have been anyone before the schism, but whatever he had done along his path, he still retained the skills. He uncovered these anew each day. A new day dawned and with it a new job and a new purpose: solve the problem.

The days and months since the interview skipped by like a flipbook but every morning Horus was reminded of the interview. At the reception desk of the main lobby sat an arrangement of lilies in squat ceramic flower pots. Sometimes there would be violets or begonias but always lilies. Two potted ficus held guard at the elevator, which Horus blew on each day to give them a boost of carbon dioxide. Strangely, overabundance of this molecule was the problem he was set to solve.

He cast away the intrusive memories and looked at the weather forecast on his monitor with the sound off. The clutter of voices in the periphery of the office jabbed at his attention through his open door. Bothersome but not uncommon. Horus locked his mind onto a series of graphs on screen. They depicted the drought's progressive damage on northern permafrost regions and the corresponding agricultural impacts. Perhaps food deprivation would make more people in power consider the climatic events shaping the world, he thought.

Horus always wanted to help even in his scant recollections of the past. Maybe the best way to help was to teach through hardship? He wasn't sure.

"No, I'm here to solve one problem. Not them all," he whispered so none outside could hear. He got the memo from his boss that read—Please don't talk to yourself so much. It unnerves some of the others. Thanks.

"Back to work."

An hour later, Horus turned to look out the window and rested his aching eyes. The smart-glass was beginning to tint as the sun rose over the town of South Moneta. The eaves of the Knapp Forest rose above the perimeter wall at the far end of the corporate campus. The leaves of oak and birch fluttered. The branches bent and bowed in the morning breeze speaking a secret sign language only known among the flora. Captured by the motion, Horus looked out the window of his second floor office in the Applied Sciences building of the American Anodyne Company and directed his imagination to create three-dimensional models of Hydrogen, Erbium, Xenon, Iron, Potassium, Helium, Europium and Radium above the sprawling parking lot half-full of electric cars.

The sunlight, which seemed to get whiter to Horus as the year went on, was absorbed by the blacktop and a series of metallic coils buried underneath the surface. The heat was transported into a liquid-salt vat for storage. At night, the heat was released and created steam for the property's dynamo turbine in the sub-levels where rows of batteries supplied power even during the upcoming hurricane season.

Horus wondered why he manifested that order of elements. None of them related to his work that day. The visualization skill, which he knew others could not do like he could, had become reflexive but this time it made him scratch his head. The manifestation felt like it came from an outside, almost alien source. Scatter, he thought, and the atoms broke apart and flew off in all directions.

With a twist in his chair, he leveled his gaze at the monitor but a tiny rainbow below caught his attention. The surface of his glass desk glimmered in a prismatic display of colors from the sun shining through the windows. Chemical engineering journals were spread like a deck of tarot cards next to an untouched green apple. He preferred to read the journals as hard copy on recycled printouts so he could mark up pages without needing to save them. Plus, using any file-sharing service through the company workflow software might allow others to peer into his interests and he didn't want that. Not at all. Okay, Horus thought, back to work. Back to carbon sequestration.

Deciding to forego the use of imagination and the possibility of getting lost in these conjures, he plugged away at a new algorithm and ran a few simulations. None of the runs presented a high enough efficiency of capture in the hypothesized solid compound. His eyes began to pulse with his heartbeat and vision doubled. Bad sign. Low blood-sugar, he thought.

He opened the desk drawer on his left below the window. There, a comb and a mirror the size of his palm sat next to a bag of stale oatmeal cookies and a bottle of eye-drops. The mirror revealed the gorged and broken capillaries on his sclera, bloodshot and tired. The green and amber of his irises darkened in collusion with the oxygen rich red blood. Can't look like I'm high, he thought, and proceeded to the bathroom down the hall where eye-drops stung as they dripped down. He peered into the mirror above the sink and hardly recognized his reflection. His face was like a toolbox with flat latches for eyes. His chin was flat and broad.

On his way back down the hall, lined with sanitizing gel dispensers on the wall, he was reminded of his first day when Luther told him the building was a renovated nursing facility that was managed into bankruptcy. When he turned into his office, a girl was sitting on his chair spinning around and around. She had moonbeam eyes and a nose like a doorknob. Green tipped blond hair tied up like a pineapple. Her blue t-shirt was emblazoned with crystals along the collar and sparkled as she spun. She was Director Mather's daughter who visited Horus on occasion to butter him up for the Halloween candy he kept in a desk drawer. There was none left, as she could have seen through the glass, so he tilted his head like a dog that just saw its master make a funny face.

"Hello, Annabeth."

"Hi, Mr. Cope. No candy, huh?"

"Sorry. No more I'm afraid," he said with a minor bow, a bow only for Annabeth, and not for the other children of the higher-ups. She was nice. Not like the others. On the very day he met the little girl, she gave up her cupcake to a small boy who dropped his on the floor. From then on, Annabeth was his reminder on how humans should behave and gave candy to her each time she visited, to her mother's dismay.

"My mom says I shouldn't eat candy. Says refined sugar is poison."

Horus's eyelids began to twitch, a happenstance of his internal thoughts trying to resolve the ignorance of some people regarding basic science, and he covered his eyes for a second and then looked to the girl who got off his chair and dusted off her jeans at the knees.

"To be honest, Annabeth, a poison is determined by dose. Refined sugar is simply glucose and fructose bonded into sucrose and it is easily metabolized. I could give you a lot of water and that would act like poison. A condition hyponatremia can be induced by drinking too much water. But it is of varied degree and causality. Other conditions can..." he said as she looked up to him with a curling lip.

That is a sign of distress, he thought, and realized he was rambling again. He didn't want to scare her.

"Oh, Annabeth, I am sorry. Water is not a poison. Don't worry. To get sick, a person has to drink so much that'd they be silly and you're not silly," Horus said and hoped she would not escalate from a condition-one confusion situation, as he designated interacting with children, to a condition-three reserved for tissues and copious apologies.

"I am silly, but not dumb, Mr. Cope."

"You are most certainly not dumb. Are you...?"

"Upset, no. Just playing. My mom might be scientifically illiterate, but my father is the head of this research department," she said, walked over to the wall and leaned, arms crossed, eyes dry.

"How old are you?" Horus asked.

"I'm eleven," she said.

"A most wise eleven at that," he replied and marched to his chair.

"That's what they tell me," she said and Horus fixed his chair to align with the recess under his desk.

"Why are you here? If you don't mind me asking. It's not a holiday is it?"

"Nope. Got suspended and my mom is not home," she said.

This information unnerved Horus more than he surmised upset her, but he had no concept or plan how to proceed. He scratched the top of his head and realized his scalp was a bit too oily and needed to buy a new type of shampoo, but he caught himself before he could go tangential. Focus, he thought, this situation must be resolved. Perhaps she needs real help.

"Is there anything I can do?" he asked and she chewed on her lower lip and sprung off the wall.

"You could do my homework for me," she said with all seriousness, but he could tell she was joking.

"I can't do that, even if I wanted to, since it would not actually help you. How about I teach you a few tricks to make learning, well, memorizing easier," Horus said.

"You can make me smarter?"

"Not smarter, you already are very smart. This just makes remembering easier. It all begins by creating stories. Humans think in story and most do it visually. We start by finding..."

An hour later, Annabeth had exceeded Horus's teaching by being able to recite more than half a deck of playing cards he gave her by using associated images and stories after being instructed in how to design a Mind-Palace. Then, he realized he had not finished his work. As Annabeth sat on the floor with the deck of cards spread across the tile, Horus got a call on his cell phone. His friend Luther's face popped up and he answered.

"Hey Luther, sorry to say I can't make it to... Oh, hi, Calvin," he said and all his muscles tightened at once as news was delivered.

"I understand. I will speak to you soon, Calvin. So sorry," he said and swiped the phone as his hand began to shake.

Annabeth looked up from the cards sensing the shock emanating from Horus.

"Sounded bad," she said.

"Yes. It was but nothing for you to be concerned about. Hey, let's go find your father. I need to talk to him anyway. Okay?"

She gathered the cards and sorted them into a neat and straight pile. As they walked toward Mr. Mather's office, a woman in gray tweed slipped down the hall in a slither of serpentine motion that reminded Horus of a woman he saw on vacation, but he knew it couldn't be her. The thought of wearing tweed in this heat made Horus itch. Annabeth went into her father's office then Horus entered and told him he needed to speak about a personal day.

...

In front of the Lawncroft Funeral Home, the lawn was thick and thriving. Perfect mowed lines. Perfect height. The edges were tight and free of debris. Even though drought conditions persisted from the spring into mid-summer, the lawn was a masterpiece of the suburban sensibility. Water was at a premium price, but the business had to keep up appearances. The backyard, where a broken-down Hearse was hidden by a pop-up tent, was dead brown. Dust collected in a thin film on the driveway and on the windowsills of the renovated Victorian home. White paint faded and flaked in the ardent sun of the summer burn.

The onshore breeze from Long Island Sound tumbled in gentle rolls across the three-acre plot scenting the air with salt and the stink of hydrogen sulfide gas from low-tide. The dirt whipped up in tiny dust devils danced across the driveway onto the side parking lot, full for a Wednesday viewing. The cars parked in even rows were already coated with a tint of pollen. Now particulates of sand and quartz cut into the paintjobs as the wind picked up. The back window of the visitor bathroom dinged with gritty air and the entity inside, for a moment, marveled at how this drought ravaged world contained such beautiful sounds.

Her cocaine curated fingernails scratched along a handheld mirror to scoop a sifted dose of Revive, the consciousness altering compound that allowed for a mental signal to break through the higher dimensions. Cocaine was only used by operatives to keep focus on the lines of reality that separated so easily while they moved through this Cognate world. Though she, designated Aerys, rather enjoyed using the human drug simply because it was there and easy to get.

The Revive, hesitant to ingestion, was bound with code to hold a viewer in a reality until the subroutine resolved and a connection was made. When snorted with a short inhalation it left a white residue like cocaine. Dried blood remained encrusted in her nostrils from weeks of abuse and made it difficult to get a good snort. The mirror slipped back into a slinky strap purse as she turned on the faucet. Before she could cleanse her nose, Horus Cope popped the heat swollen bathroom door open. She was a lemur in the night, big eyes, clothes black and white, stuck in a fright.

Behind Horus, the faded years of the funeral home stood in contrast to his eyes bright with fury. A terrible confirmation of all his worries and doubts was betrayed by his unblinking stare. Red eyes glared with anger but then looked down. His hands thick with callouses reached for his face low with weary. He rubbed the dark circles under his eyes and took a deep shuddering breath. She turned off the faucet and he lifted his hard gaze from his hands.

"Everywhere I go. There you are. Even in grief, you follow," he said.

"That is because you are nowhere," she said and pulled out sunglasses from her bag that then covered her eyes like twin eclipsed moons.

"That's what you always say. Even in my dreams," Horus said.

"You don't dream."

"I remember you."

"That's the problem and now you must see Hexifer again," she said and crossed her rail thin arms across her chest, bag dangling against her narrow waist cinched by the mourning gown.

"I know that name," Horus said as confusion twisted his brow in both a statement of fact and wonder.

Horus looked down for a moment to the white tile floor of the funeral home's private bathroom. The summer sun poured in through the window, which was etched into a scratchy haze from years of harsh New England weather. As he looked back at the woman he had seen throughout his entire remembered life, she merged with the shadows like every other time and was gone. Like every other time.

A gentle wail bellowed through the hall to remind Horus why he was there. His friend Luther. He was a hard man to like with his constant boasting and tendency to say inappropriate things even if everyone else was thinking it. A memory of Luther on the stony beaches of Nantucket, corralled by steep dunes, kicking the sand at Horus's book as he sprawled on a worn beach towel.

"You need to get out of the fantasy world, man. See that sand, it's real. That book is not. Look out there. Sun. Sand. Ocean. All waiting," Luther said in a fast fleeting memory.

Even though crude, Horus thought, he was right.

An assistant funeral director, a hawk of a man, latched his bony talons on Horus's shoulder and said, "Mr. Cope, it's time to go." Not sure what was real, Horus figured he should deal with the task at hand. Burying his only friend, or at least the only friend he could remember. He took a solemn step, shifted, and shuffled down the carpeted hall. The orchids, white and delicate, cast a scent that causes Horus to sniffle. He hated his allergies more than the parasitic flowers. A thought thread about epiphytes began to unroll in his mind, which he soon terminated. Distractions would be disrespectful and that was the last thing he wanted. The last thing.

As he reached the viewing room, the casket shut. Luther's family, like a flock of ravens stunned by grief and most likely alcohol, began the procession to the cemetery.

Horus could not feel the heat of the deep summer, humid and petulant, but the sweat caused a rash on his neck at the back of his collar. No scratch would end the itch. The last word was said about Luther and the family bowed their heads to pray but he would not. The tumble of fresh cut grass and dry pine needles carried on the breeze. The scent of salt was gone. Now, so was Luther. Down in the ground.

From behind the granite mausoleum where the cemetery's gravel road turned toward the rising hills, a man with a yellow beret stood. His thin black suit, a black so dark that it seems that no events or space could occur within it, flapped in the wind but he remained still. With a single blink of his folded eyes, he stepped into the narrow shadow cast down from a cloud above. Where he stepped out, the shadow followed.

Horus could feel his heartbeat in his eyes when he saw the figure and his hands trembled. He did not know why as there was no reason to fear. All sound vanished, not even the cries from Luther's family penetrated Horus's ears. The man stopped his stride and he shook his head so that the beret fell to the ground. Horus's eyes tracked the hat and when he looked back, the man was gone.

You're losing it, he thought, and he then realized Luther's brother Calvin was approaching. His full sensorium returned in time to hear Calvin ask if he was going to the lawyer's office to hear the reading of the will. His head shook no and scratched the back of his neck.

"I don't want anything," Horus said and began to walk away to his car.

"He left you his..."

In a blink, and a half breath, Horus was driving down the highway not knowing how he got in his car or where he was going. Time had been lost before in his life and few memories from before remained, but this was different. This was a jump in time.

"Horus, Horus, Horus, is that what your name is now?"

He flashed a look to the passenger seat and saw the man from the cemetery but now his suit was yellow and his beret was black.

"Great," Horus said and all he could feel was an empty pocket inside his chest where his heart and warmth should have been.

"Couldn't save this one either," the man said and Horus bent the wheel, pulled off the highway, and slammed to a halt. Skid marks painted the road.

"I know you now."

"Of course."

"I forget everything else, Hexipher."

"No, you don't, not really. It is all stored. Oh, time for a test," said Hexipher with a half tilt grin betraying pointed teeth like cracked quartz crystals.

Horus thought, losing it again, talking to myself. That's all. Just hallucinations like before. Just need my Clozapine.

Hexipher let out a sigh and said, "That look. That sagging defeated look. This is the thirty-fifth time I've had to say this but here we go. You are not crazy. Time to prove it. Boulder."

Over the berm in a wilting corn field, a mound rose. As if the earth were giving birth, a boulder the size of a small car popped out. It began to roll across the field and flattened all in its path. Friction caused cracks and craters appeared on the surface. Horus yanked the seat belt but it would not release the clip. The boulder began to gather speed and jumped the berm onto the highway. A divot cracked the asphalt and the mass began to spin towards the car. With a flurry of tugs and muffled cries, Horus fought to flee.

"Stop the boulder," Hexipher said

The boulder came close enough for Horus to recognize that the object was a facsimile of the moon and it was picking up speed. Only a few seconds were left. The seatbelt was frozen. There was nothing Horus could do, in a last resort of confused neural firing, he threw a punch at Hexipher's thin angular face. He thought the blow would disentangle him from the elaborate hallucination, he instead shattered his knuckles. Hexipher's chin did not budge. The boulder cast a shadow across the windshield.

"You're kidding," Hexipher said and looked forward at the imminent crush, "You passed the protocol threshold and unlocked a shibboleth but no actualization."

The headlights of the car shattered in an explosion of fine particles as the hood creaked under the mass of the rolling stone.

...

Thump. Thump. Thump.

Blood pulsed through overburdened veins on his temples. Pain coursed through the skin on Horus's forehead. Eyelids, heavy, not wanting to move, fluttered and hazy light separated into streaks. A slit of sight widened into a crescent of dull vision. A clack filled his ears. Then another. And another.

Pushing up, gravity compressed around him, or at least he felt it that way. He buckled before attempting again. He sat up and as his sight cleared. Horus found himself in his bed. The black satin sheets, soaked with sweat, wrinkled on his legs. The clacking continued but he saw nothing around that could make such a racket. Hard sunlight pitched in through the window shades and warmed his feet at the foot of the bed. Everything seemed to glow even though each item from wall to ceiling to carpet was black. The lacquered sideboard twinkled like obsidian in the expanse of eager light. A queasiness trickled through his veins and into the pit of his stomach. He never, even while intoxicated, opened the shades. The clacking sped up and he looked up. There, lounging, outstretched, on the ceiling was the Hexipher tapping a cane in the air, though it struck nothing, the clacking resonated through his bones.

"I do envy the dormant modes, sometimes. Quite a nice escape," Hexipher said and descended from the ceiling with a slow rotation down to the ground. His feet landed on the dark hardwood floor with a soft and deliberate touch. Horus knew no hallucination was so persistent and active in sight, sound, and even smell as the room wafted in odors of licorice.

"I give up."

"Good, good, that's the first step," Hexipher said and smiled as his eyes moved apart ever so little, but enough to send chills down Horus's back.

"Go ahead and kill me then."

"Not going to kill you. Can't even do that here. It is time for you to get on with the process. Time to level up," Hexipher said and his eyes moved back into their previous bird-of-prey like positions.

"I don't understand."

"Not supposed to understand it all, not yet. There's no fun in that," Hexipher said and stepped to the foot of the bed.

"If you can't tell me," Horus said as rage spiraled through his being, "then get the hell out!"

Strain squeezed Hexipher's face and he was pushed back by an unseen force towards the door. He began to giggle like a child who was licked on the face by a puppy.

"There it is," he said and froze in place.

Horus shook his head and slipped over the side of the bed.

"This isn't real."

"Yes and no. You are real. The place is real to you. But, nothing is really real or not nothing among the Cognate Hierarchy," Hexipher said.

With that, Hexipher lifted his cane over his head to a high-guard, crooked his neck, and leveled a narrow gaze at Horus that bent with intent, an intent practiced and old.

"Stop me."

The cane gleamed and the round shaft fell away to become a blade. Hexipher stuck out his tongue. The sound of a thousand shrieking crows echoed through the room and he struck. A silver flash cut through the air. Horus threw up his hands without thinking and all went silent. There, an inch away from the crown of his head, the blade.

"Finally," Hexipher said and tossed the blade into the ceiling above.

"I still don't understand."

"In this phase, you are only to accept and relinquish. Now do us both a favor and relax. The transition can get fuzzy," Hexipher said.

"Please, just tell me what's going on."

Hexipher looked stunned.

"Please? Well, well, you have come a long way. Never in any of your priors have you said that word. Okay. You are from somewhere else and you committed a few troubling acts, so you are going through a process of enlightenment. Your ego got the better of you, so penance will be made and I lead you through certain phases. Sort of like that Virgil character in Dante you so liked."

"I never read that," Horus said.

"Oh, that was in a prior. My bad. Didn't leave you with that memory. So, in each Cognate reality, you are real and so are few others, but mostly the others are sui generis simulations. Ever think other people were just automatons or like you are the only real person in the world? Well, it's true in a sense. There are some others. Now, you fulfilled your goal in this world. It was to accept that you cannot control everything and that you can fail. The test is complete as evidenced by your restoration of virtual manipulation of sensory object manifestations"

"But what, am I going to die?"

"Transferred is more like it. Be happy, you only have a few more terrifying phases left. Learn the lessons and find freedom. It is that simple. Say goodbye to this place. You won't remember it. Mostly," Hexipher said and placed his hand on Horus's forehead. It felt cold and dead to Horus. He resisted his want to recoil.

"What about my work, my friends, my life?"

"That's where you will go if you succeed. One lesson at a time. One aspect at a time until you are reformed," Hexipher said and closed his eyes and the scent of licorice filled the room.

"What if I don't reform or fail?"

"Then I get to delete you in the most horrible way possible."

Hexipher opened his eyes and a bubble of space expanded between them to fill the room. A vision of vast ocean flowed in the space and drained into a horrible void.

"Lastly, if you fail. The others will suffer."

All imploded into a single point and became a roiling sphere of absence. Hexipher stepped out of the singularity and into a room, a perfect cube with amber walls. The phantom operative, Aerys, resolved in layers as if being printed by a ghostly 3-D printer.

"Excellent work, Aerys. You triggered his next cycle right on time. Was getting bored watching from the planck," Hexipher said and slid up to her without moving his body.

"It's what I do. Let me guess, a Zgornian cyber-beetle chaperone? No, a Vermille bounty-hunter with a tesseract hive-mind?"

"Neither."

"So I won't be tracking or watching our friend?"

"No tracking. You will be exactly as you said though. A friend."

"Really? Hominid form again. Dull."

"Best be off and no more cocaine."

"Not like they'll have it where I'm going."

"You know what I mean."

"Fine, but if he doesn't level quick, I'm glitching the whole construct. There isn't time to hold his hand. The convergence comes, and the trial will not be fun."

"He's the one who created the mess. Time for him to get the mop."

"Sometimes trying to get through to you is like throwing pennies at a train."

"Choo. Choo."

Transference 3.145—The Wheel.

On the northern ledge of the floating city of Aval, a synthetic iceberg where more was contained beneath the waves than above, Heron wiped the salt spray away from his aberrant green eyes, which no other has in the iso-colony. The filament thin tracker band coded to his bio-sig clung snug on his wrist. Awaking from his dormir-vault but a few days prior, he had yet to gain his ocean stance to combat the surge and swells, but most important to the other occupants, especially the Trans-Mogs, he had yet to be Blessed. Heron was assured this would happen once his permanent living quarters were arranged. Somehow, he had ended out on the rim of the floating city. A place called the Ring.

A vague memory of another ocean circulated in his mind, making the scene familiar, but he could not shake the foreign feeling to the circumstance as if it were a future dream. Trying to reassure himself, he took hold of a section of railing that ran along the ledge except for the opening a few steps away where individual watercraft were launched. Just one of many breaks in a ring where a staircase eased gradually to the dark water. At the base, lotus kelp bobbed up and down with their star shaped petals catching the energy of a lowering sun. He realized he was standing on a dock and too close to the water's edge.

Along an array of cone shaped buoys about a hundred meters off, a pod of dolphins chased a dispersal of flying-fish that skipped off the white-cap waves. He could feel the front of the storm sorting through this stretch of ocean from east but had no idea how. Heron rubbed his hands together and clapped. No echo or reverberation called back. The sense of empty depth inside him was reinforced by the endless sea. The sun, a blood orange dripping faltering light, bowed to the west and sent a stack of crepuscular rays through bulbous clouds, racing to meet the curve of the planet, across the white polymer deck of the city's north promenade.

The surface of the floating city was but a cap on a black mountain of living plastic bobbing on the salt driven currents. Heron knelt and touched the pitted flooring as a series of small waves impacted. He began to tip backward and tripped toward the inlet slip for the watercraft. He found himself tumbling faster, uncontrolled like a top losing angular momentum, to the edge and the deep blue below.

A hand grabbed his shoulder and tugged him back to the safety of the inner walkway. Heron thought his eyes deceived him. A raiment of blue fire poured down over a figure from a wide basket-like hat. Though knowing he should say something in thanks, he could not force the words. He was stunned in more ways than one.

The hand released him and the figure countered the sway of the plank below as if made from water and fire itself.

"Come on. The Ring jetty is no place for nodders," said the figure and led him through a tight alley slick with spray over the smooth plasticized surface. They stepped through a hazy blue light barrier and onto a street cluttered with servoid robots going about slushing up muck. The blue fire envelope dripped away from the figure and ceased. Underneath the basket hat, a human with the skin of a dolphin and eyes of an octopus wrapped in a purple kimono.

"Wonder who let you out? Nodders are to be netted in the estuary," the figure said with a mid-range voice neither high nor low. The heft behind the volume was impressive to Heron. It cut through any creaks of the servoid servos or the rhythmic thumping of the wind above on the surrounding domes of glass and plastic. Regaining focus, Heron bowed to the figure.

"Thank you for your assistance. Forgive my lack of knowing, but what is a nodder?" Heron asked.

"You silly. A sleeper recently awakened."

"And the dock, why is it so unstable under foot?"

"The Ring that surrounds Aval, which uses the kinetic energy from the waves to generate electricity. Pretty place to watch the sea but unstable unlike the rest of the city."

"May I ask your name?" Heron said as he lifted straight.

"I am Ludwigia. Lucky for you I always go on a walkabout after free-harvesting the kelp beds in the pools. Otherwise you could have been food for the lotus," said Lugwigia. Heron watched as the octopus eyes changed from shimmering yellow to green and reduced in size.

A metallic orb half the size of a person rolled up to them on the street. A holographic projection of a human who reminded Heron of a frog resolved.

"Good to see you two have been acquainted. Now, Heron please come to the Temple of Tesla for culturation. Ludwigia, escort him, and feel free to answer any question. CEO Andronc out. LOL" the hologram said and blinked out.

"LOL," Lugwigia replied.

Heron was confused. More confused than he surmised he should be.

Ludwigia waved him on and began a quick but measured stroll toward the interior of the city. A few blocks away, they entered what seemed to be a market district but empty of customers. Heron caught up to Ludwigia. A bit out of breath, he posed questions that rattled his mind while trying to read the geometric script of the signs glowing above a storefront of glimmering glass.

"I am all out of sorts. Much of the terminology is lost," he said.

"Please, what can I help you with?"

"When I think of the letters C.E.O., the title of Chief Executive Officer comes to the fore and LOL means something about laughter," Heron said and Ludwigia stopped.

"Close but it is Chief Existential Officiator. Andronc is the one who will be testing you. LOL means 'live on land'. It's an ancient benediction but since you don't know it you must be old as dirt."

A bit offended but wasn't sure if he should be, Heron scratched his head and came to find that he did not have any hair.

"Old as dirt, huh? Guess so. Sorry, what?" Heron asked and Ludwigia crossed her arms across the silky purple kimono. Heron noticed that the exposed skin had gone from a gray to a dark tan.

"The Time of Dirt when the ancestors lived on land. Before the ZB's drove us to the sea. You must have been put into stasis then," Ludwigia said, spun to the street corner, and pointed, "Let's go. The TOT has all the answers."

"Temple of Tesla?" Heron asked and smiled. Ludwigia smiled back.

The walk was not long but time stretched out in the barren corridors between domes, cylinder towers, and buildings made of bubble clusters covered in iridescent dragon scales. What never left was the taste of salt on the air. Heron managed to get a couple more answers. The blue fire that flowed from the basket hat was cold plasma and stopped UV radiation. Ludwigia was one of the last Fluids, which meant an ability to alter the body with adaptive genetics and nano-cellular agents. Most were lost in the last conflict though Heron didn't ask what the conflict was. He was glad to have questions that could be answered as others ravaged his mind. He knew there was a time when he could see atoms in his mind and that there was something more.

Andronc was not a pleasant frog-man. Or that is how Heron chose to think of him. Squat. Skin tinted green. Eyes like eggs stained with coal. Slimy. Slimy on the inside. He did give off the scent of bergamot and cinnamon, so Heron found that nice, but added to the confusion. In an office on the tenth floor of the Temple of Tesla tower, Heron sat in a smooth chair of plastic just like everything else in the city. Holding the hand rests made his palms itch. Great, he thought, I'm allergic to a city.

Andronc hopped up from his scoop of a seat and over his lumpy desk made of viewing screens and holographic projectors. He landed in a heap by Heron's feet.

"Going to make this clear as the sterile seas of the south. We woke you because we need genetic diversity. Seems we are lacking. Our scientists say one mutant disease or improper coding could lay us low. You are the oldest we have and thus the most untainted DNA. But, and this is a great big but, you will need to go through a few trials, and if you fail, well, then, we'll simply need to rethink this whole revival of the "ancient ones" deal. We can make do with a sample of your DNA but proof is in the putting," Andronc croaked.

"Pudding. You mean pudding. Originally it was 'the proof of the pudding is in the eating' but was changed," Heron replied, wondered how he knew that, and scratched his palm.

"What the trench is pudding?" Andronc asked and hopped back behind his desk.

"Food. Never mind, so where do I go now?" Heron asked.

"To the dorms with the others. Ludwigia will meet you there. I have made arrangements."

The dorms were underneath the waves in the below decks. In the egg-sack like growths off the hull of the plastic city, Heron peered up to the rippled and undulating surface. The light fluttered and washed through. Gleaming dispersals of photons penetrating the water column. Crepuscular waves of light twisting above. He lowered his chin and extended his gaze down through the portal to the benthic regions below. The deep called out a dark urge to him. His mind seemed drawn to the abyss, but he shook his head to clear his thoughts. He had to orient to this new life. First, figuring out how the gel bed worked and then the toilet. The hose that extended from the bathroom floor with a pulsing, hungry flange was a bit unnerving. He longed for a solid hard porcelain toilet but the memory and image washed away.

His front door, only door really, irised open. A man, and Heron knew him to be a man by his nakedness, saddled inside. The man had a bulge protruding from his forehead. He grinned and then sneered. Heron though the man might poop the floor from the strain on his face but Heron was in luck. Until the headache.

The man kept staring and Heron rubbed his temples in pain. It hit him. He was being hit. Hit by ultrasonic waves. The man was doing echolocation. Heron put up his hands and screeched back in the highest pitch possible, "Stop!"

The man's narrow slit of a mouth sucked to a pit. He turned away. Obviously in pain from Heron's shout.

"You want to know something, ask," Heron said and sat down with a squish on the gel bed.

"Sorry, sorry. Wasn't sure if you could understand me since you're a dirt person," the man said and came back around. His arms went akimbo and he stood there with his genitals dangling like dead tube worms.

"The dirt thing. Gotcha. I understand you perfectly. What do you want?"

"To see if you really were as dense as they said."

"Dense? I only just awakened and people are calling me stupid," Heron said and flashed up his arms.

"No. What? Stupid? No. Density. You know, how much matter you got packed in there. I am sorry. My name is Vib," he said.

"I am Heron. Nice to meet you, Vib. I wonder, could you possibly put on some clothes. We dirt people aren't used to gents pacing about with their bits all a pendulum. And please ask before sound scanning me," Heron said.

"This is going to be odd. Quite quite quite. I like you, Heron. For that, I will wear clothes tomorrow when I begin training you. I am pleased though. You are far more intelligent than I supposed for a dirt person. Won't be like training walruses at all. Poor things. All went extinct about fifty years ago. All right then. Tomorrow," Vib said and shuffled out into the intestine-like hallway.

Heron thought, why did he wonder about my density?

Little fanfare or ceremony followed Heron through the guts of the city the next day after a fitful sleep. The gel bed protruded from the wall like a transparent curling tongue giving Heron the distinct impression it was trying to digest him. Passing through a few sphincter doors that closed as veiny valves, Heron realized they were bulkheads as a multiple-hull ship might have in the long gone past. The mixture of biological and polymer architecture was difficult to accept. Heron followed a robotic sphere-guide through the intestinal tract to the lifter tube. He stepped in, and upon sealing, he felt his inner ear compress with pressure. In a pop, he was tossed up and out of the lifter onto the surface of the city like a plug from a cask bobbing up and down in the ocean.

The Blessing was rather anticlimactic. Inside what appeared to be a hollowed out jellyfish, Heron waited and a weak gush of air dusted him with glitter. The semi-metallic compound sunk beneath his thin skin. He felt nothing. The process was a simple absorption of intelligent nano-particles.

In a garden lounge, Heron found Vib and Ludwigia waiting for him. An array of dune grasses and saltmarsh reeds circled the lounge based on a deck-work of polished wood. Sand corralled the edges of the platform. A long bench beset with heart shaped cushions curled around and in the center of the platform a palm tree rose two stories. A gentle aroma of sandalwood floated about.

A serene scene to be sure, Heron thought, but then a shrill rose in his mind. His head began to ache. A great hand seemed to squeeze his forehead. Vib sat and crossed his legs. Heron was glad the man decided to honor his promise and don garments. From memories hidden away from another time, Heron identified the clothing as a wetsuit. Gray and foamy. Giving Vib the form of a mammal born to life in water and on land. Vib kicked his dangling leg a few times in a restless gesture. Heron began to look around and the city beyond, once empty of human life, patches of haze resolved and soon the haze became distinct forms of bipedal humans shuffling about.

"What the blazes? Where did all those people come from?" Heron asked and took in a slow deep breath to tamper the pain. The ache released in a pulse and cleared his sight.

"The Blessing allows connection to all. Before, you were partially linked so we could interact. Now, your sensory input is cast through the ON. Except tactile input. That got messy long ago. Sharing sexual activity at inappropriate times made it hard to get work done. Plus, the poor asexuals got forced to sense things they never asked for," Vib said and swung his leg back to the ground.

"The ON stands for Omniscient Network. It exists only within the city proper and lets you see the people cloaked in dust-fields, the totality of the Blessing. It does not extend beyond that blue barrier you saw out on the Ring," Ludwigia said and took his hand. He was engulfed by the scent of citrus. Bergamot, orange, and lime all at once. He had a craving for a fruity cocktail. For some reason the name Margarita popped in his head. He banished the thought and focused.

"I was wondering about that. Considering the sort of welcome I received and lack of orientation, there is much keeping me in the dark. I assume this has to do with the purpose of my awakening," Heron said.

"Bright for a dirt person. Yes, you and Ludwigia are the last of the ancients. Andronc told you our need for your DNA. This was true. Our hierarchy is faltering a bit but this is not the only purpose. Others will come for you. Once there were five cities like Aval and many small conurbations like archipelago, but they have gone the way of the hive and threaten to destroy our way of life. You will be the source of our protection. If, you survive the testing," Vib said and clapped his hands together, "Right. On to it then. Let's see what you got."

The first test was easy enough. Running around in a chamber where holes would spring leaks and a variety of materials and objects scattered about that were needed to stop the room from filling up with cool seawater. It was uncomfortable in the wetsuit garment they had him wear but the slip-on shoes were a nice fit and did not grant blisters to his heels. The second test was accessing the ON and finding landmarks within the city. It took Heron half a day to enter the flow of information and find a way to display a map after going through countless files with an alphabet he never encountered. Though it looked like morphic pictograph cryptology, how he knew that he couldn't ferret, the language reset after each file was opened.

The last test of the day was simple. Heron figured it must be a joke when he was tossed over the Ring and into the ocean. All he had to do was swim back to the quay through the rolling swells. Problem was, when he hit the water, he found he did not know how to swim. He did know how to sink. The current slung him away from the deck.

The water had a grip to it. Slick. Constant. Bottomless.

And it pulled. And Pulled. And Pulled.

Heron thrashed and fought when water ran up his nose and barreled through his throat to his lungs. The water burned in airless breaths. Having no fat on his body and long limbs that cut through like a bow, his descent gained speed. Panic cut away into action. His hands stopped paddling. His finger outstretched and cinched together. The salt of the water that stung his eyes went away when he closed the reluctant lids. Calm came when he fought no more. Heron halved his mind and let the sympathetic nervous system go.

The darkness was fond of hallucinations as most would know but it is also conducive to wiping the slate of the mind clean when given the chance. Heron did that. If he died, at least he wouldn't need to navigate this strange world he had been awakened to without any context. Then, a plan arose. With coordinated rhythm, hands cupped and drove down and then his feet kicked. He forced out the water from his lungs and tied off the panicking part of his mammalian brain that wanted to rage in a fit of survival, which would have him end up dead. Silly contradictions, he thought and pushed his way free from the grip of the water. The surface loomed with washes of sunlight dappling the tension above. Just a few more meters. Then a mat of material drifted overhead. A bed of lotus kelp coming in for the kill.

Heron stroked his way to the ledge bobbing up and down in the swells but the kelp matched his path. A tangle of tendrils swayed in the water column looking for prey. A small fish swam too close and was speared through. The mass of the kelp closed around the fish but a section detached and followed Heron. He could do only one thing.

He took off his slip-on shoes and pushed it at the near side of the kelp. A tendril sprung out and coiled. Heron took his other shoe and pushed it toward the other side and it was coiled as well. He knew the predatory kelp would soon discover the shoes were not food. Heron emptied all his energy and swam like an injured monkey towards the surface. He popped his head through the surface and took a deep inhale. His damaged lungs protested but he got that surge of oxygen he needed and made for the quay. He could sense the lotus kelp turning and coming after him. He pitched his head to both sides and saw two other masses converging on him. His hands slapped the water.

Out of breath and on the verge of unconsciousness, he sprinted to the rising and falling edge of the platform. Panting, he slipped up on the deck and pulled up his feet in time to see the kelp merge below. Victorious adrenaline pumped through his veins and he did the only thing he could think of. He urinated on the kelp below and laughed. The kelp immediately sank.

"What the blazes?" Heron said and Vib came up behind him.

"Nasty kelp sure doesn't like piss. Think it is uric acid or maybe the ammonia compounds," Vib said and tossed Heron a towel.

"Could have told me that," Heron said, dried his head, and tossed the towel back.

"Wouldn't be much of a test now would it," Vib said and waved for him to follow.

"You're an asshole," Heron said.

"What's that?" Vib asked and picked up the pace.

Back in his chamber, Andronc and Ludwigia waited. Andronc looked gassy, bloated, even for a frog-man.

"I think the last test is a formality, but nonetheless it must be done. Then we can formulate a DNA bomb to disrupt the hive-mind attackers. Maybe even bring them back into the hierarchy," Andronc said and hopped over to Heron still dripping with seawater.

"Can we do it now? Get it over with?" Heron asked.

"Why not," Andronc said and waved his webbed fingers across the air. The lights went out and a virtual room resolved where there was a red carpet with black fringe. In the middle of the carpet was a ball. Andronc stood beside Heron. The others were gone.

"This is an ON matrix site. All very interactive. Your test is to get the ball without stepping foot on the rug," Andronc said and croaked.

Heron shook his head. He walked to the edge of the carpet.

"You must be kidding," he said and began rolling up the carpet. He reached the ball and picked it up. "There. But there is another way, a more satisfying way." He rolled the carpet back and patted his hands clean.

"No one has ever defeated the challenge alone," Andronc said and gasped as Heron took hold of the frog-man and hurled him at the ball. Tumbling end over end, Andronc hit the middle like a billiard ball. The ball rolled off the carpet and Heron snatched it up.

"That was more fun," Heron said.

"That was what I thought you would do. That is how every one of us has won the challenge before but not by rolling up the carpet."

"Telling. Very telling," Heron said and the room disappeared.

Back in his chamber, he sat on his gel bed and began taking off the wetsuit.

"You all need to find a better way of examining your awakened citizens," Heron said.

"This is how we have always done it," Vib said.

"That is your problem," Heron replied, "Now get out."

The days and weeks came and went. No sign of the hive-mind attackers but the season was changing and ominous pewter horizons worried Heron. One morning while sitting in the garden lounge with Ludwigia, who had become more of a friend than before, he voiced his concerns. Ludwigia told him of the new season. The season of wind and clouds where they would need to run on reserves since the sunlight would be diminished. Not much of a worry. They had the wind collectors and wave impactors with that hearty piezo-electric crystal that generated volts with pressure. Plus, during this season the Wheel provided enough to run the robots, the medical facilities, the labs, and agro-vaults. They went back to Heron's new chamber in the Bubble-Rise building a few blocks away after a nice meal of seasoned kelp and synth-pro. The sexual encounter was more acrobatic than Heron was accustomed but he did not complain. At the end, the city seemed to shift like a fault line breaking. A creak rumbled the floors and Heron thought it was part of their act when Ludwigia ran to the window. Heron turned and made his way to the window that was more eyeball than pane of glass. Half of the city, from the glimmering dragon scale domes to the sleek towers of rose quartz cladding, was in shut down mode. All surfaces reverted to a matte gray.

"Power is down. Not good."

...

A salamander of a person, Utkia, came to Heron's chamber and ran the summoning bell. Three chords in E minor ran through the chamber. Andronc's replacement was a more patient and steadfast being less prone to emotional displays when status was concerned. Heron liked Utkia and liked that they answered his questions more directly instead of constantly answering questions with a question like an amphibian Delphic oracle. Heron even bowed to Utkia when they entered wearing a scarlet jumpsuit, which seemed to move like living blood when the eye was looking away. Heron offered Utkia a drink.

"No need for that," Utkia said.

"I hope I earned my place and am not to undergo any more tests since you have my DNA to make a viral contagion bomb?" Heron asked but really stated.

"You are an honored and official member of the city. I come seeking help. We have a problem not encountered before and hope you with your fuzzy and liquid thought processes might come up with a practical solution," Utkia said and a thin tongue slithered out to taste the air.

"The Wheel?"

"The Wheel. It has been frozen for three days and without the power our labs will not have power to manufacture the DNA bomb in time. We don't know how to restart it. It has been going for three centuries without fail," Utkia said and slipped down into the swinging chair made from wicker and fronds. A special item Heron made while bored.

"Get me the plans," Heron said.

Hours burned like the sunlight casting over the horizon. Heron examined the holographic layout of the structure. He flicked the image and it spun like a wheel of fortune landing on an ugly fate. When it stopped, he pointed to the opposing teardrop shapes on the spoked ring like flat bumps on a tire. The mechanism was simple enough based on a water-wheel that sat below the surface of the sea where waves could not batter it back and forth. Two tethers bound the great structure from a central hub down to the seafloor many kilometers down. Expanded, the artifice was sturdy and lashed with thick coils of corrosion resistant materials. A metallic glass from what Heron could derive. He zoomed in on one of the bulges on the ring. He was amazed he didn't recognize it before.

"That's a submarine. Two in fact. Balanced on either side. What are the means of propulsion?" Heron asked and scratched the top of his bald head.

"Buoyancy. While one descends and fills its ballast tanks, the other ascends and pumps out the water. The air rises. The Wheel turns or so I know," Utkia said and a tapered tongue lashed out and cleaned their left eyeball.

Heron zoomed in on the descending submarine and took interest in the curious structures at the fore and aft. He pointed to the front of the submarine.

"The propeller is in front," he said.

"More like an impeller but yes. It drives the internal dynamo to create electricity for its pumps. Or so I suspect. None have been inside so it is all speculation. The pipe extending from the tail, also speculation, is the outtake where buoyancy gases are expelled along with ballast water. The intake is secreted along the hull on the underside. I suspect."

"Let me get this straight. One submarine fills with water and generates force by sinking; thus, driving the impeller that in turn creates electricity. This electricity is used to activate pumps that intake water and get rid of it. This would make it positively buoyant and rise. This occurs in opposing fashion in each of the submarines depending on the upstroke or downstroke cycle of The Wheel's rotation driven by these attached submarines," Heron said and took a deep breath. He bit on his lower lip and lolled his neck back and forth. Motion soothed him during recent times and he couldn't fathom how this came about. Perhaps it was the Blessing but there was still much being kept from him.

"Indeed. A gravity-buoyancy engine turning another. The axle connects to the dynamo in the benthic level by rotor and is intact and in perfect order. The submarines have stopped. If the problem arose here on Aval, we could fix it. Not there. Have any thoughts?" Utkia asked and pressed up off the seat and sauntered over to the hologram.

"Numerous. The batteries could be corroding. A hull leak. One of the fan-blades to the propeller, I mean impeller, could be warped or fused. Maybe entropy finally got to the system. The problem with perfect balance is when one thing stops so does the other. Maybe by overcharging one of the submarines, the other could be kickstarted. Might overcome the stall."

"There is a buoy, a solar powered one that has a cable, but not long enough to reach either," Utkia said. Heron mimed putting his hands in his pockets, his pants had none, and kicking an imaginary ball. Something did not add up for him.

"Only one thing to do. Go in the sub and look around for the problem," Heron said and looked to his bulbous window. The horizon grew gray.

"Some have tried. A scan prevented entry as did countermeasures. That was a decade ago. None bothered since. It was only a novelty after all and no threat to the hierarchy," Utkia said and the scent of warm honey and browning butter filled the room. Heron found it emanating from Utkia.

"You smell. Don't get me wrong, it's nice but you didn't smell that way before," Heron said.

"It's my dinner alarm. Got to go," Utkia said and rushed towards the door. Heron waved his hands, "Hey! Hold on. Why not just talk with the hive members?"

"They are hive and we are hierarchy. They do not value status, station, and order. We cannot co-exist. Either we change them or destroy them. I really must go," Utkia said and the door grew a membrane after they exited.

That was what I was afraid of, Heron thought. Humans of Aval had specialized so much that predictability reigned. Humanity had once been an amalgam of those who sought structure and easy to understand pathways to life and others who placed more on egalitarian explorative lifestyles. This allowed small groups to survive. Factions of balance. When one became dominant, the cohesion of the social groups broke. No advancement without risk but too much risk and disaster could befall them by not being cautious. What an incarnated contradiction he stood inside. Perfect balance had seized The Wheel and imbalance had created a chasm too wide for the societies of humans to close. They no longer cultivated adaptability to each other. Though he did not know enough about the hive-people. Perhaps they were dangerous, but he did not want blood on his hands or brainwashing.

There was only one other he could discuss this with but the ON connectome would pick up on their conversation and visions. Luckily, Ludwigia and he found another way to communicate. He needed advice.

Always being on ON was a drag. Sure the medical benefits of being dosed up with nano-machines scouring the blood for infections or repairing skin damage from one hour too many in the harsh UV of the promenade was nice. Knowing that all was seen and heard was frustrating when one simply wished to bathe in peace. None of that bothered the population of Aval except Heron. In the long ago, when he was something else, privacy was a popular currency of the wealthy. For a short time at least. During the acrobatic bouts of intimacy, Heron and Ludwigia found that they could use touch to keep secrets.

They tested out their discovery by writing short sentences on each other's palms. They amped up the frequency and possible effrontery. None was responded to by any authority or challenge. Heron realized the ON connectome used them as sensors and did not copy their conscious thoughts. They were relays and monitors. Everyone was everyone's keeper. Now they could jot communications that dissolved as fast as thought in short term memory. It did tickle so Heron had to learn to keep composure; otherwise, he would become suspect.

In the hanging garden in district 13, Heron and Ludwigia sat under a row of palm trees and held hands. Unseen, messages were written and replied. Heron began the last sequence.

The flotilla of hive-people is to be here after the season of wind.

Yes. Power problems do make a mess of things.

Most appear not worried. Like they have many protections.

There are more weapons than they let on.

That is what I fear. Change or death.

Then change death.

What?

We are not them. We can choose.

Choose what?

Something unpredictable.

A helpful ruse.

To what end?

A new beginning.

Are you going to do something dangerous?

If I can figure out how, yes.

...

Not one person from Utkia to Vib tried to talk Heron out of his plan. In fact, no one bothered him at all. He figured they got what they needed from him.

Getting the submersible launch was easy as walking to the benthic level bay and taking one. It was clasped between two sets of massive tongs above a pool of water. Heron slipped over to the cigar shaped tube. The burnished aluminum exterior shell was texture in violation of the smooth plastic and glass body of the floating city. A periscope reached out a meter from the dorsal surface like a mantis shrimp eyestalk. The aft was a single magneto-dynamic fluid accelerator and vectored 360 degrees to give the capsule a full range of motion. The fore was flat with a recessed face of three meters where a gap could be created when attached to a solid plane. Not a vessel of speed but one of slow deliberate movement and the fore acted as the docking hatch, which created a pressure seal on other surfaces allowing for egress. Being large enough for only a single person, Heron opened the side hatch and crawled inside. He spun the manual bulkhead lock. A hiss of air signaled an airtight seal.

The interior was a nest of soap bubble foam that formed to fit Heron's body. A single control stick sat below a dangling pair of goggles. He signaled to ON and the craft launched through the pool and out into the depths. Through the goggles, Heron saw the vast stretch of water that he had to cross. He followed a series of cogs and cams along the connecting rotor from the dynamo attachment port on the subsurface. Each cog got bigger to transfer speed to the facility in RPMs. Finally, he meets the single rotor rod that speared to the central span of the massive spoked wheel. An image was conjured in his thoughts of an amusement park, no, a place along an ancient river where buildings glittered in the sun and a Ferris Wheel sat. The city of London popped into mind but then it all vanished. The submersible set a parallel course to the center of the The Wheel's hub and axle. There, he would then make a correction to the target submarine. A good scan of the surroundings was needed to get a better picture of the intents and motions of the massive object. A waterwheel under water driven by gravity and buoyancy. Kilometers down, the creak of water pressure groaned. Strange low-frequency booms penetrated the hull. Stories of sea monsters and ancient mariners streaked through his mind. From where these stories came, he had no clue.

An hour of descent passed but the targeted submarine came into view. Heron was doubting his decision. Perhaps he should go back. Everything was still so strange. He was betting on a single element. One difference between him and the others that would allow entry. But even if he could get in, could he fix the problem? After that, the ruse had to fall into place. That was for another time. He had to concentrate on the moment. The fore impacted the submarine with a resounding thud as if a spoon clacked against a heavy pot full of soup.

A wave of force pulsed through the cabin of the craft. Minor arcs of electricity hopped from bubble to bubble cushion. Heron felt his mind surge. He saw a tunnel of fractal light and then his fears melted away into a warm slick pool at his feet.

"Electro-Magnetic field. Strong. Almost strong enough to erase memories. But I think it freed some," Heron said out-loud not knowing why. He didn't want the ON to hear even if it was out of range. There could be remote drones or some other devices.

"Yes, it was and don't worry. They can't monitor you here. Come on in builder," said a voice both in Heron's head and in the cabin. They combined into a chord. A minor chord he believed.

A portal irised and pulled the submersible inside. The water pressure equalized and was siphoned out. The whoosh of air filling the void tinged off the hull of the cigar craft. Lights flashed. The bulkhead opened and Heron wriggled out. The air was stale but breathable. A minty tang came across but perhaps that was the EM field messing with his mind, he thought. A door slid away into the neighboring wall to reveal a seat on a conveyor track. The chair reminded Heron of a barber's chair. Strange since he was bald after all and couldn't remember if he ever got a haircut. He plopped down on the chair and it spun forward and zipped down the tracks. It came to a halt in a command center where a figure was surrounded by visual monitors flickering about. Some in static and some showing the sea. What concerned Heron was what else he saw. The figure appeared to be glued to the hull as if a giant spider spat webbing across their body. Then he realized it was fiber optic cable. A cybernet.

"Been waiting for you," came from everywhere in a tin voice.

"Thank you. That's very kind. I am Heron," he replied.

"Always with the H names. Vain bastard."

"Excuse me," Heron said as he scanned around the vessel's command center. No chair except the one he rode in on and no lights but the monitors' lambency.

"Sorry, been here in this tug for a long time now and was getting rather bored. Want to leave so I stopped moving to get your attention. I knew it would work after your last lesson," the tin voice said and crackled into what Heron could only assume was a laugh.

"Your name?"

"ARSS. Automated Recycled Synthetic System, but you can call me Aerys. On to biz shall we?" the tin voice solidified on the last word. More brass than tin now.

"I would like to know what is wrong," Heron said.

"Nothing. Just tired of going in circles. The systems are fine. The ballast pumps, the prop generators, the batteries, all good. Water comes in and I go down. Batteries charge. Water is pumped out and I go up. Over and over."

"We need you, please, to start the cycle again so power can be allotted to the city. A season comes where our solar stations are down and the Buckminster windmills will be unstable. I humble beseech you. There is more hinging on right now than just a need for more power. There is a reckoning," Heron said and bowed to Aerys.

"You mean you're going to restore power so a DNA bomb can be detonated over a fleet of people because they don't want to be rigid butt-puppets," Aerys said and the bronze tone hardened to steel.

"Butt-puppets?"

"Sorry, sorry. I get a bit testy at this depth. But you are going to attack them?"

"They think they are. I am here to restore power so I can then sabotage the DNA bomb, but I need more time, and they need to feel a sense of security. I mean to start a dialogue. Join the two estranged principles."

"No shit? This is different. I was supposed to be your friend and tell you the story of how you created the nano-tech that took over humans and made them into mindless solar powered zombies. You did it for a good cause. To save the planet from the floods but you didn't cast your prognostications far enough. Then, you couldn't put the genie back in the bottle and didn't fix the climate problems. Blah blah blah, you helped get nannites to collect all the plastic in the oceans and build the atolls and cities. But, ZB or solar zombies went nuts and began hunting for nutrients instead of planting themselves into the soil. Did I forget to mention that? Sorry. So everyone had to move to the rubber boats and to survive had to reprogram themselves to be well, what they are now. With your help of course."

"I did this."

"Yup. But at least you want to fix it in this iteration. Kinda sucks. No temptations. No pleading. Well, what's done is done. Hexipher!"

"What? I know that name," Heron said and felt the air pressure in the submarine increase ten-fold.

"Of course, you do," came from the shadows of the corridor, "Next phase."

The submarine winked out of existence. A sphere of amber light replaced it. Hexipher in a hybrid crow-mechanical man form tapped his cane and Aerys still as a Cybernet plug-in undulated in the air like a bobbing buoy.

"If we leave him alone, he does better," Aerys said.

"I don't want him too. He needs to suffer more. As he once told us, stories are the real coding to humanity's minds. Only stories can undo stories. His penance isn't done," Hexipher cawed.

"Don't think it's your choice anymore. Just got a signal in from the Cognate. The intersection is coming. Got to get this resolved pronto or trillions of possibles will never get to be coded souls."

A set of black wings rose from Hexipher's back. In one beat, they were gone.

....

Under a dome made of black-body tiles, formed a sphere of energy designated Node-100 Bulk MV-5. It hovered and emanated a starlight glow next to four other spheres of equal size and luminosity. They revolved around each other in gyre orbit of synchronicity and syncopation. A channel of particles bound with error-correcting codes flowed in from one side to another in a ring and exited the opposing side.

In the dome, there was an arcade structure of light and matter with a vaulted ceiling, buttresses, and a series of holographic chambers along long stretches of concourses. From a certain point-of-view it appeared to be a metal beam gantry like one from a human factory overlooking a manufacturing floor. But here, there was no central floor. Just an abyssal absence surrounded by walkways. A trail chamber sat lodged in a walkway on the top-level concourse with five sim-universes. The chamber resembled a single room schoolhouse on the outside, but within were the universes that spun like shimmering discs connected on a spindle.

An even dispersal of light formed a haze of illumination in the chamber except where the black body tiles consumed the radiation on the interior walls. In the middle of the room, stood Hexipher in true form. Its body was human, but where there would be flesh, there was translucent plasma. Sparks flowed purple and cerulean streaks charged with internal energy were trapped in by a thin invisible skin so smooth it created no friction, which only became apparent when the Hexipher turned his head. Five rotating platter shaped cores of internal light spun next to him hovering at waist level. The light haze next to Hexipher churned and became absent, a void of darkness formed. Aerys stepped out and bowed to Hexipher. The void snapped shut.

"It is the closest to the terminal point, the real terminal point, you have sent him. They might be able to detect me," Aerys said.

"Yes. They will detect you as planned," Hexipher said and eyes formed on the surface of his featureless face.

"I must protest. There are no drugs there that can keep me focused. I will be integrated into the physics. Worse, they might make me do chores," Aerys said and stepped back as a column of light formed between them.

"You will do what I say. He cannot be allowed to atone and elevate. Yet."

"Just destroy him," Aerys said and her human form begins to tremble and vibrate.

"I am governed as you are governed. I cannot enter the Cognate worlds unless he triggers the cascade and then can I torment him, but only during transition. You can interact, but not fully unless you are integrated. And so you shall be a witness."

"I won't be able to escape," Aerys said and the body fell away into particles of dust to reveal a skeleton of lines of operational code.

"I will retrieve you. Remember the internal time-dilation. What would be an eon for me will be but a moment for you. Go."

Aerys stepped into the column of light and the beam bends and poured into MV-5.

"Let's see if you do better with your son this time."

Transference Specularis: Intersection

The tortoise shell hills of Litchfield County meandered below a wide and long country night where they grazed upon the Earth. The stars bloomed with lustrous radiation in a meadow of indigo sky, which had not seen such a clear Hunter's Moon in decades. The red flicker at the belt of Orion appeared again and began to grow until it consumed the empyrean twice the size of the moon with a thin crimson illumination. This unnatural star appeared to violate the depth and width of the canopy. The curl of round noise like a dog's howl bark that never broke penetrated the region where electricity no longer held sway. All knew Betelgeuse was not dead but might soon go nova . That was not the case. This was more like a bubble breaching the surface of the sea of time and space.

Hermes Sojourn swept back the curtain to his cottage window overlooking his weathered and warped porch. The false star popped and was no more. A white light of regret began to burn inside him.

As the sky resurrected the proper night, Hermes opened his front door. A creak of old wood and rusted hinges announced him to the silent landscape of his overgrown estate. His forty-five year old knees cracked when he stepped out to survey the split-rail enclosures beyond the gravel driveway where horses once frolicked. Nothing but grass swaying in the breeze.

"Damn quiet sure gets loud," said Hermes and he ignited his kerosene lamp.

Getting hot in hand, he picked up his pace and ambled over to the corner of the porch. He placed the lamp on a white toilet used as a table. Not many fireproof items existed anymore and a stroke of luck was the only reason he found it among charred remains of a house. He turned the gas off deciding that the stars would be enough for his watch. He didn't have much of that type of fuel left.

He thought it was colder than it should be this late in the spring. The chill pressed and his scratchy turtleneck sweater did little to defend him. Five-day stubble caught and pulled on the worn wool. He slid down onto the spindle rocking chair that no longer rocked, an old athlete that no longer runs. The scent of a hardwood fire spiked with resin from a neighbor's chimney rode the cold currents and drifted by Hermes. Recollections of him and Roquetin stoking the family hearth only a year ago flashed and faded.

"Well boy. What are we going to do? Guess I'll just sit and wait a bit longer."

He couldn't tell if the moon was rising or setting. All he knew was the deep country sky that surrounded him broke his heart more than the night before. Now steady in the rocker that no longer rocked, he looked to the cedar shingles on the façade of the cottage gray and broken. It was where the double-barrel shotgun leaned. The only thing keeping that barrel out of his mouth was the bottle of Laphroig scotch standing guard next to him. Hermes knew they would cooperate one day.

A hard-edged breeze cut through the property, overtaking the fields, and sliced across Hermes' blanched face. A decent sleep had not come calling in weeks. He rubbed his hands together and then touched his cheeks.

"At least the cold hasn't changed."

Pinecones loosed by the wind tumbled to the ground from the spruce next to the cottage. The rustle grabbed his attention while the moonlight bent around the porch banisters to form slats of shadows before the two front stairs.

The shades became darker and pooled together as Hermes caught sight of the phenomena.

"Intersection," was said out of the pooling shadows.

He leaned to the shotgun as the shadow spilled upward. Two figures in the shape of humans undulated back and forth. Ripples shimmered across the apparitions black as ocean trenches.

"What are you?" Hermes asked.

The shadows grew and defined arms and legs. Flat faces like sheets of carbon fiber turned when Hermes grabbed the gun. He took aim at the lurking specters.

"Get away," Hermes said as the forms approached.

"I'm warning you. One step and..."

The shadows took a step. The muzzle flash tore through the nebulous beings. The blast echoed through the hills. In an instant, they reformed and Hermes slid towards the door. He reloaded and bore down on the motionless shadows. A screech came from the phantoms. The shrill lacerated his ears with a violence of bells and splintering wood. The pitch rose and the volume jumped. He fumbled with the doorknob when a dark hand lifted and pointed. The shrill ceased.

"Convergence will destroy you all. Find the key and find your son. Stop the end," the shadow said.

"You know where my son is? Tell me," Hermes said. The other shadow lifted its hand and touched the other being. They merged into one mass that began to dissipate as a swirling cloud.

"Not ready," said the shadow.

"Tell me. Where is he?" Hermes yelled.

"Unworthy."

"Fuck you, unworthy," Hermes said and shot the shadow.

The smoke began to clear as did the ringing in Hermes' ears and he heard the fleeting words, "Find your son. Find salvation."

His eyes rolled back into his head and he collapsed onto the deck. The gun fell from his grip and knocked over the bottle.

…

The shotgun blasts echoed through the hills and alerted Ross and Carrie Mulder. They had moved to the hills before the day when the internet went away. That was decades ago. Never had they heard a gunshot in real life before. Now, they heard them every other day. They grabbed their rifles from the wall mounts and slung on their matching barn coats. They raced out the door. Ross was a vortex of a man. Always in motion. In rotation. Calm in the center. Violent on the edges. He grabbed a solar charged flashlight from the mailbox that hasn't seen mail in over five years. He mounted it on his rifle site. Carrie already had the other flashlight set on her gun. The twisting marl road crunched with deathly dry gravel under foot. They swept back and forth like so many practiced times before.

Each kept one eye on the uneven road and one eye on the lookout for marauders rumored to be in these parts since the harvest.

Carrie's night vision was better than Ross's, so she kept a stern look along the underbrush where it was easy to hide. During the day, her eyes gleamed with a disharmony of jade but at night they appeared black. Their flashlight beams tracked and bounced up the road towards Hermes's estate. They scanned across the cottage. No movement. Ross and Carrie rushed closer. Ross raised his rifle and nodded to Carrie to circle the house. They swept the perimeter to find nothing but a cold wind laden with hardwood smoke from home fires burning over the ridge. And the faint repulsion of skunk. As they converged on the porch, Ross held up his hand. Carrie stopped. She angled her rifle to the ground.

"You smell skunk?" Carrie asked.

"Yeah. One of Harrison's hounds must have gotten sprayed again. All clear," Ross said.

"Clear," Carrie replied. Ross then spotted Hermes out cold.

"Herm is down," Ross said.

There was nothing. Not even darkness. Then Hermes felt a sting zigzags through his mind and distant mumble. The mumble defined into his name. His eyes struggled open. There was Ross's face weary with an Ivy League education that no longer mattered. Hermes sat up with a fast twitch that sent Carrie a step back.

"Herm, what happened?" Ross asked. Carrie sniffed the air. The fragrance of misery, common among the community, tingled in her nose and directed her eyes to where the bottle spilled its aqua vitae.

"Ross. He's at it again," Carrie said as Hermes begins to push up to his feet.

"Herm, are you getting shit-faced again?" Ross asked and shook his head.

"No, no. I'm not drunk. Don't have that luxury anymore with the roving packs of monsters about," Hermes said. Ross curled his lip and bit down with a sort of anger that came with broken expectation.

"You know if you keep doing this no one is going to check on you. The Harrison's have already banished you from their property and told everyone at the meetings to not bother. You don't even come to the meetings anymore and you're the one who started them," Ross said.

"You can't just go and shoot your guns for no reason, Hermes. We're all running out of ammo and you're making us more anxious," Carrie said.

Hermes took a full deep breath, scanned his property with suspicious eyes and lifted his hand.

"Listen, I didn't even have a sip. I think I fell asleep out here or was sleep walking," Hermes said.

"In the cold with a shotgun and a bottle?" Carrie asked

"I know it looks bad but come and smell my breath if you don't believe me," Hermes said. She did.

"Satisfied?" he asked.

She nodded.

"Come on inside. Can't feel my hands," Hermes said.

After explaining what he thought was a dream, the three sipped rosehip tea at his kitchen table covered with plumbing fittings and small wrenches. Ross and Carrie looked at each other and shrugged in unison.

"Not like my dreams haven't become more disturbing since we were forced to leave the last gated town because of the riots," Ross said.

"This has been hard for all of us," Hermes said.

He wondered how a Wall Street investment type and his younger socialite wife ever survived the upheaval but let the thought slip away.

"Tell us why you stopped coming to the meetings?" Carrie asked.

"Roc is gone. He's the one who made me do what I did. Now, I'm working on something else," Hermes said and sat back. He lifted his teacup and blew. The steam swirled away into gossamer curls that vanished just as the people's lives once did.

"You going to tell me about it?" Ross asked.

"About what?"

"About what you're working on," Ross said.

"Maybe when I have more done. Going to town to trade some copper for car batteries tomorrow. Do you two want to join me?" Hermes asked.

"We were going anyway to get mail," Carrie said.

"Good."

...

Hitched to a rail fence, three New York carriage horses, long retired, were saddled. Ross checked all straps and bridles. The young morning cast a yellow warmth across the verdant hills though the chill remained low on the ground. Steaming breath escaped the horses' flared nostrils. The brown coats shimmered with a glossy iridescence. Ross brushed the matriarch Sally with even strokes on her legs corded deep with muscles. Hermes sauntered up lugging a few copper pipes in a faded blue bed sheet. They clanged a chorus of discordant dings. He thought that Ross and Carrie could run the region soon if his project failed. They had the only functioning horse farm. Ross bought as an investment, which gave the greatest return of Ross's life; their safety.

"You're early," Ross said.

"Couldn't sleep after last night. Figured we could make good time and get back before the sun starts climbing down."

"I'll get Carrie then," Ross said.

"No need," Carrie said as she came around the barn with a rifle slung on her back. Her black winter jacket, designed for arctic weather, held her snug. Her work boots kicked up dirt gray from the night's freeze.

"Let's go," Ross said.

Down at the fork of the shared gravel road where their properties adjoined, the asphalt road, Mountain Laurel Drive, glittered and betrayed the ice not yet sublimated by the rising day. Soon, the asphalt would crumble away like almost every other road of the region. The rhythmic clop-clop, clop-clop, of the horse's gait lured Hermes into a daydream. A vision of his son, Roquetin, before he left wearing his Giants Superbowl Champion hat, conjured through his mind.

"No more games," Hermes said. Ross, who was riding next to him on the shady side of the road, looked at him with a raised eyebrow.

"What?" Ross asked. This word broke the trance and Hermes came back to the cruel present.

"Nothing. Was just thinking about football," Hermes said.

"Damn. I miss it too. The Jets would be AFC Champs right now," Ross said. Something happened that Hermes didn't think could happen, a smile. A twisted, sarcastic smile, but a smile nonetheless.

"And the Giants would be Superbowl champs after beating them in a rout," Hermes said and snickered.

Ross did just one simple gesture to reveal his thoughts. At that moment when they reached the intersection of Mountain Laurel Drive and Roxbury Road that lead into town, Carrie pulled the reins and brought Sally to a halt. The men caught up fast. They flanked her as the steeds shook their heads as they stopped.

"Recalling the past is good and all but I suggest you two focus on business. We need feed and you need batteries. There's going to be a lot of people congregating today. So be mindful," Carrie said.

"You're right Carrie. The trivial things don't matter anymore but they are hard to forget," Hermes said.

"Before we get back on track, are you going to tell us about your project? You can't just withhold. I know what you can do," Ross asked.

"Since you know about me and haven't revealed who I am to our neighbors, I have an offer. Fifty-fifty, if I can get things going. Help me, combine our property and we might just return a bit of civilization to this place. You in?" Hermes asked as his horse began to stir and rear up.

"Woah, Seth. Woah," Miles said as the horse's hooves clacked on the road. From around the bend, the deep thump of a diesel engine descended and scattered through the bare woods. The vehicle would be upon them soon.

"Into the brush," Miles said.

They spun, galloped single file until they reached a row of thick pines flanking the road like a legion of sylvan stoics, and went off the road. Sheltered behind the wall of trees, they calmed the horses with calm voices as the vehicle got closer. Hermes held the pipes tight so they wouldn't make a sound.

A screech of tires spiked the air. Fright loomed behind their eyes. The car stopped. The engine idled with menace and a door opened on Roxbury Road.

"See anything down the road we can use?" said a deep male voice that boiled like mercury but Ross, Miles and Carrie dared not look and reveal themselves.

"No boss. Just dirt paths," said a young man's voice eager with anger.

"We'll come back and check later if this shit-hole town has anything of value," said the boss.

Sally began to stir and in turn made Seth snort. Carrie rubbed the horse's mane and settled the horse's nerves. Ross pulled a .357 revolver out from the inside of his barn coat.

"You hear that? Should I go see what's down the road? Could be deer," the young man asked.

"The bullets we got are for people. Now, let's go case the town," said the boss.

The door closed. The engine became enraged with dark diesel fuel. It screamed as the car left black streaks and headed towards town. Puffs of dirty smoke hung on the air.

"We need to warn the others," Ross said.

"There were only two of them from what I could hear. It'd be suicide if they tried to rob anyone in town. Nothing to worry about if we weren't on the road," Hermes said.

"Let's keep our guns visible to scare off any potential highwaymen," Carrie said.

"Agreed," Ross said and continued, "So what's the project?"

"Not now. I'll tell you after we deal."

The clatter of horseshoes on the broken pavement alerted the inhabitants of the town now called The Intersection where two routes crossed at the compass points. Hermes led the others to a makeshift market set on the old town green next to the Post Office, which was thatched with dry vines scaling the brick walls.

...

In the meeting hall where loads of letters were sorted and stacked on warped fold out tables, the talk was of phantom towns, Brigadoons, appearing where ruins lay. Stories of ghostly Visigoths in mechanical armor pocketed the discussions. None could explain what was happening and some of the older folk lamented the loss of search engines on the internet. Back in the days before the Great Burn, information flowed fast. Hermes reminded them how much of it was propaganda or misinformation used to sell products no one needed. Still, he longed for the ease of information as well.

He knew what caused the tragic event. Him. Never would he disclose this. He would be impaled or worse. Ross had some idea but not the whole story. They were better off he thought. All the information on nuclear weapons and the ways to launch them was gone. No more could they set fire to the sky and fry every circuit with an EMP.

His plan was to restore civilization, but slowly. No one could stop the climate events set in motion so living in the hills beyond the reach of the risings seas was best. He feared if he rebooted the world too fast, they would continue on the same path, and no one would survive. He went back to the market and bartered what he could. The sun was beginning to descend so he went back to the stall. Ross and Carrie were not there. He went out to find them. He turned the corner and the scent of horse manure was strong and tangy. He grimaced and went around the corner towards the Main Street.

A hand grabbed his shoulder. A spike of fear ran down his neck and he spun. A girl with a blue bonnet held up a letter.

"For you, Mister Soujourn," the little girl said. She handed it over and skipped away down the cobblestone alley.

The letter dropped from his hand when he finished reading. His son was alive but taken by a group of ghostly Visigoths near the remains of a place called Avon. He could no longer save the world. He had to save his son.

...

Hermes took a bite of an apple as he strolled the corridor of his underground bunker. A vast vault of storage lockers took up the eastern wing holding all the lost technology he could hoard before the incident. The walls were meters thick concrete with layers of lead sandwiched inside. A vapor barrier stopped any leeching and an industrial dehumidifier prevented any moisture where molds, mildews, or bacterial colonies could take hold. The air was therefore dry as a salt desert and tasted of powdered stone from decaying cement.

He passed by the rows of hydroponic bays and the seed vault. The apple had begun to brown and soured his enthusiasm, so he tossed it into a wall shaft that hurled it down to a composting cistern closed by a negative pressure valve. The lights came on as he entered his office. The only high-powered computer within a thousand kilometers was glowing ready. The terror of success coupled with the consequences of failure weighed him down in his work chair. The sightings of the phantom towns, people, and now the apparitions that haunted him were evidence enough that part of his experiment came to pass.

The laser platforms and the implosion devices sent to the Lagrange point did something to upset space-time itself. They wanted to see if they could access the underlying geometry of the Calabi-Yau dimensions and pass a message to another universe. Problem was that the security was too weak to stop the

Neo-Anarchs from hacking a portion of the imploders and only half arrived at the determined point. The others had been wrested away under a meta-material mirage-cloak the military devised and a false signal replaced them. They thought all the devices were accounted for until the boom and the silence when all unshielded circuits fried.

Hermes realized his problem besides the weak security protocols. They were trying to punch through space-time when they should have tried to burn through it. The elasticity of space-time could hold the mass of suns. What were they thinking? It would be like throwing a bowling ball onto a trampoline when they should have just taken a bit of acid and put it on the fabric of space-time and burn through. Vacuum friction was the key.

He had the portable equipment: lasers to create optical tweezers, EM bubble containers, and the proper elements to create an array of spinning silica balls. Lugging it up to Avon would be risky but it was the last place his son was seen and where the Brigadoon town had surfaced from nowhere. He might get a message through with the right opening. He could negotiate for his son's release. He was certain the experiments outside the atmosphere destabilized local space-time but the other reality had the means of traversing. He just had to get a message to them but he had to do it alone. Couldn't risk any of his new friends.

The computer ran his simulations. He went up to his porch and waited for the morning to dawn. He wrote a letter to Ross and hoped he wouldn't do anything rash. If he didn't return within three months, the bunker would open for

Ross and he could carry on his goal to revive civilization again. No shadows fell upon his watch. The sun was coming up.

Avon was a lovely region of the former Connecticut. Besides the burned houses and the ancient trees toppled across the roads. Hermes came across a few bands of people living nomadic lives under spring-frame tents. No signs of the incursion from another reality but some people had stories about a lightning bolt that froze into place by the town hall every week or so. None dared investigate. It was hard enough hiding from the marauders and highwaymen. The town center, or what remained of it, was full of them. Now the tent people were going to the Farmington River to head south and follow the small creeks and streams to the old Yankee Expressway before the winds of the early summer clogged the aquatic artery with branches and bodies.

Hermes had forgotten what time of year it was but the scent of pollen bourn wildflowers and sweet honeysuckle affirmed the season. The hyper-canes, even far offshore, would pummel this area with barrels of wind all the way north to the desolation of Montreal. The carbon sequestration technology was working before they accidentally let conspiracy theorists blow up the world. This is my fault too, Hermes thought and slipped off the road when the chug and chunk of an engine came from behind.

The soot of diesel twirled by his nostrils but the vehicle stopped before the bend in the road. The engine dopplered away. Must have been a scout team, Hermes thought. Better pack away my gear and do some reconnaissance.

Being holed up in an abandoned bakery a block away from his target, Hermes noticed a cut on his arm was infected. He couldn't believe he didn't bring any antibiotics along. It was stupid of him. Even if he didn't need the medicine, he could trade it for just about anything. He cleaned the wound the best he could when a paralyzing force pinned him to the dust covered floor. A monstrous flash of light filled the second story room through the cracked window. He wasn't sure, but he thought he smelled ozone over the aroma of yeast metabolizing somewhere in the bowels of the bakery. It must be the frozen lightning phenomena. But, he couldn't move. The force released its hold and set minor distortions in the walls as it passed through. He crab-walked over to the window. It wasn't a single frozen lightning bolt. It was as if two of them struck and formed an oval portal. Through the portal three figures exited. A haze surrounded them in an aura.

He couldn't believe his eyes. There stood Roc like a god descended from Mount Olympus. Fear was dashed. Hope bloomed. He rushed down the stairs and out the door.

"Hey!" came from behind as he ran down the sidewalk that was clean of any trash unlike the rest of the town.

Half a block away, Hermes looked over his shoulder. Three men in hunting camo were trailing a few feet away.

"Roc! Roc!" Hermes shouted and waved his hands.

Confusion crimped across Roc's face. In a motion so smooth it must have been practiced thousands of times before, Roc drew a pistol and pulled the trigger. No bang. No sound. A pulse slammed into Hermes' chest and he was unconscious before he hit the ground.

Hermes didn't know how much time had passed. It felt like he slept for days. Cramped and drowsy, he woke up. His stomach rumbled. He knew this only happened when he hadn't eaten for at least a day. His eyes opened to slits and around him were bars. His son had imprisoned him but he was not inside a building. Odd light fell around him.

The jail was low tech. A cage of iron and nothing more sitting in a recently mowed glade between two strange forests. The leaves were massive scoops and almost black. Too round like spoons. Hermes sat up and shook the bars. No loose joints or welds. He wasn't getting out. A bowl with a thick blood red liquid huddled in the corner by a mustard yellow loaf of bread. Or so he thought. The clouds thinned above and the sun warmed his shoulders. A bit too warm for his liking and he shielded his eyes as he glanced to the sky away from the sun. The spectrum was wrong. Too much orange. This was not his world.

A cracking twig betrayed a presence in the forest. A hundred and one terrors could inhabit this world, Hermes thought. Could I be bait for some sort of hunter's trap? Perhaps an ambulatory fungus with symbiotic viruses? Then a strange memory came forward. One of a floating city and a tale of zombies made from humans and nanobots. There was little else he could do besides think. The shuffling of feet grew louder. The shadows of the trees hid a solitary figure. Bipedal and lean. The figure stopped and stood there.

A scent like lavender and lemon drifted in the air. The scoop leaves whistled like seagull cries when the breeze picked up. The whistle chambers in the leaves vibrated and pollen lifted off from curled stamens. Hermes realized the trees utilized the mechanical qualities of soundwaves to aid in reproduction. The wind picked up and the figure stood hidden. The whistles climbed in volume until the surrounding forests seemed to be screaming at each other. Hermes plugged his ears.

The figure stepped out of the shadow. It was Roc. He could tell from the cleft chin, ears like violins, and large forehead but faceted goggles clamped on his orbital sockets that reminded Hermes of wasp eyes. Roc held up a thin but rigid sheet of plastic the size of a hand tablet. The transparent film roiled and swirled with squirts of light. Tiny fish swimming into signs and symbols Hermes could not recognize.

"Roc, it's me. Your father," Hermes managed to say with a hoarse voice. He didn't realize his throat was so dry. He stood up in the cage and waved through the bars. Roc tilted his head like a confused dog. The air around him crackled with static. A shimmering shield formed around him. The distinct smell of ozone wafted by Hermes. Roc was upon him in a flash. Then, perfectly still, Roc stared at Hermes through the wasp goggles for a moment that stretched Hermes' stomach. This was all wrong.

"Roc, are you okay?"

Roc said nothing. The wind died down and the whistling trees went silent.

"Roc, it's me. Your father. I've come to rescue you," Hermes said and reached for him. A pain ran along his arm when he contacted the shimmering shield. Electric and sharp. He pulled his hand back and gripped his wrists. He wriggled his fingers to see if they worked. They did but were numb.

"What's wrong?" Hermes asked.

Roc held up the plastic sheet and waved his hand in a rolling manner indicating he should continue talking. Hermes pointed to his mouth, "You want me to talk? Why?"

Roc tilted his head to the other side. Hermes understood that he didn't understand.

"Okay. I get it. I'll talk. Here's the story of when I first took you fishing at Lake George and you cried because we couldn't take any fish home as pets."

An hour later, the plastic sheet glowed a glorious purple and blinked three times. Roc wrapped it around his wrist and the film was absorbed into his body.

"I can understand you now and speak your language," Roc said.

"What happened?"

"That is a better question for you to answer. How did you cause the convergence?" Roc said and Hermes knew at that instant this was not his son.

"I don't know what you're talking about."

"Yes, you do. You look like my father but that evil man died in an experiment to open Bulk Space or so we thought. I scanned you, and you are not him, but you are him from the other reality. Meaning your paths are linked. I bet you had the same consuming interests. What did you do?" Roc said and lifted his goggles. His eyes speckled with flakes of metal and a transparent nictitating membrane winked.

"We tried to open a micro-wormhole with imploders, nukes, and high-powered lasers all set on a focal point but sabotage caused a calamity. We failed. Nothing happened. Well, our planet almost died but that wasn't from the experiment."

"The experiment took place outside of orbit, didn't it? Past the Luna and in the gravity flats of the Grimmer Range."

"Yes, I think so. The names are different but yes. Why?" Hermes asked.

"That was where our largest Dart Reactor was stationed. It was all safe. Chirp Lasers pushed hydrogen along at speeds until they collided with boron. No radiation or excess heat. Capacitors held much of the charges expelled and so did some orbiting battery arrays. But then a warp twisted it and released the energy all at once. A fracture grew and enveloped my world. We stabilized some of the damage but soon entropic fields manifested and stole every erm in those effector ranges. Our world is now out of balance and we must restore it."

"How can I help you?" Hermes asked and folded to his knees.

"You already did. The how was all we needed to reclaim our purloined substrate."

"This doesn't feel right. Your technology is more advanced," Hermes said.

"By about a hundred years and we never had the accident you caused."

"Now that you have your answer, can I see my son? Can I go back?"

"We are in a preserve where no technology is allowed. After I go back and fix things, you can rejoin with your world," Roc sneered. He inched closer. The look in his metallic flecked eyes told Hermes they sought revenge.

"Can I see my son?"

"You already have. Seems the multiverse doesn't like when duplicates meet in a single reality. I touched him and all he was joined with me, but not his mental information."

Hermes sprang to his feet and gripped the bars. The warm metal became slick with his sweat. "Do you have any of his memories?"

"Memories do make the man but sadly we mostly forget the past and he is the past," Roc said and leaned closer. His electro-static shield crackled with contact with the bars.

"What will become of my reality?" Hermes pleaded.

"Reality will be just fine. Your planet though is another story. After we siphon off what we need, it will most likely fall into a darker age. Maybe even an accelerated decay of elements. The highest probability is it will die. Like your weak son," Roc said and began to pivot. Hermes snapped his arm through the bars and was struck with the shock of the field. He endured the pain and grabbed Roc.

It was over in a blur. Hermes had yanked him back so hard that Roc was unconscious after striking the bars. The electro-static field grounded when Roc was pinned down but not before sending a massive charge through the framework. Some of the weld softened and Hermes broke free. The only thing left was to run.

After days of crouching, creeping, and crawling along the forest boundary, he found an outpost. A lightning portal like the one he came through was energized and being emitted by a massive arch that was of a substance he had never seen. It was veined with streaks of metallic tendrils and was pulsing from opaque to perfect clarity. Must be a metal-glass, he thought and watched. He timed the patrols and the sentinel shifts. He then had his opening. He would get home and fix his world.

The guards were going through a shift change and Hermes ducked. He ran from cover to cover and reached the final stretch. He wanted to explore this world but there were problems to solve. With every last ounce of strength, he went for it. He felt his heart pound in his chest and eyes. Vision narrowed to slits. The ozone smell began to overpower his senses when Roc intercepted his path and held up his arms. Only fifty yards away. Hermes pushed on.

"You were wrong, father. You were wrong," Roc yelled.

He knew it was a trick. Calling him father would not stop him. He clenched his hands into fists and pushed harder. Roc's head tilted. He shook his head. He grabbed the sides of his face and then looked at Hermes like he did when he got lost at Lake George.

"I'm, I'm sorry I didn't say goodbye when I left," Roc said.

What? What? Was his Roc inside fighting to surface? He made the decision and plowed onward. Roc braced knowing what would happen.

"No, no…"

Hermes tackled Roc and hauled him up. He flung them both at the gateway. Roc punched his back.

"I was lying. Stop," Roc said but it was too late.

They tumbled through the lightning portal back to the center of Avon. Roc was dazed. Hermes stood up and dusted himself off.

"You're in there. I know it," Hermes said and heard the rumble of a diesel engine ignite a few blocks away. Roc stood up and his shoulders slumped in defeat. His eyes glistened not in sorrow but in a way that indicated an allergic reaction. Redness bloomed across his sclera.

"You are just like him. Selfish."

"You don't mean that. Come on, you're in there, let's go home," Hermes said.

"This is not my home you ass."

Roc ran at the portal. Only a few steps away from exiting, the lightning fizzled like a wire contending with a surge of power. Roc jumped but bounced off the passageway. He scuttled back on all fours.

"You've killed me. The reclamation has begun. I can't be here," he said and each atom of his body lost their atomic bonds and became a swarm of dust that scattered in the wind.

Before he could break the shock and flee from the marauders, a crow circled down before Hermes on the broken and gritty asphalt. The crow looked up and cawed. No, not a caw. A laugh. A human laugh. The crow gained mass and transformed into a figure that Hermes instinctively knew. Hexipher.

Time froze around them. All scents and sounds vanquished. A strange woman appeared in camo from around the corner unaffected by the time-stop. She came to a halt in front of Hexipher and grimaced.

"Trial time?" Aerys asked.

"Yes," Hexipher replied and huge black wings sprouted from his back.

"All according to plan?" Aerys asked.

"Indeed."

With one downstroke of the wings, the world curled away.

…

Inside a single-room schoolhouse saddled with wood pews, Hexipher stood at a chalkboard. Three questions were written in block letters.

What can you control?

What is sacrifice?

Why?

Hexipher raised his cane and swiped it over a nebulous clump of a man sitting in the front row. The man took on Hexipher's form in mirror fashion.

"Your memories are returned. Before we begin, do you know who you are?" Hexipher asked.

"Yes."

"Good. Let's begin."

The schoolhouse door opened and three men shuffled inside along with Aerys. The three men were Horus, Heron, and Hermes. They strode to the front and one by one sat down on the man's lap and merged with him. Aerys, in a suit of living chains, slithered over and sat in the front row.

"Answer the first question," Hexipher demanded.

"In a deterministic world with inviolable laws of physics, limits are set. Limits mean determined outcomes that can be predicted. If they are predicted, they are determined. But not always can we predict. We have variety and the illusion of options but no real choice. Each moment of the present is reliant on the past, which is recursive back to the moment of birth of which we do not choose. Each decision is made from what we had learned and cannot be otherwise. Only by having the power to manipulate the initial conditions, can we control anything. Even knowing everything is in itself a limitation of choices. To know all means to be bound by it."

"Sloppy but correct in your case. Number two."

"Sacrifice is necessary. Sacrifice is the movement from childhood to adulthood. Sacrifice is what I did not do."

"Correct. This is going far better than last time. Proceed," Hexipher said and jumped up high almost to the ceiling. A wood podium appeared under his clawed feet as he descended. He perched on top like a crow watching for signs of prey.

"Why? Why not. But that's not the right answer you seek. I did it because I forgot who I was. Now, I have been reminded."

"Correct! Finally. Only the five hundredth run through the historicals. So depressing those realities. Had another five to go before we implanted in a prison universe for eternity but we are done," Hexipher said.

"I killed my son," the man said.

"Yes, you did. The past you who opened the gate to this realm in between realms didn't until the last run through, so it is a yes and a no. Though it did happen that way before your transmission and rendering. Enough. I'm tired of this," Hexipher said and landed before the man. A cane appeared in hand and struck the man. The cane passed through the body and down onto the bench. The body became a cloud of living code and swirled around Hexipher. The cloud condensed and streamed into Hexipher's narrow eyes. He shuddered for a moment and the black crow form shed like molting feathers. Hexipher became a figure made of lilies, translucent flesh, and mercurial light.

"Nice to see you again, boss," Aerys said.

"Nice to be back. The reintegration was a bit itchy. Now you need to get that Revive problem under wraps or into a prison universe with you."

"I have it under control. Just don't send me into those historicals. Ancient humans make me so testy," Aerys said.

"Fine. Do what you wish. I must go find them."

Walking to the next nexus in the hub took the equivalent of 10,000 days but Hexipher reached the Vault of Ages and Memory #10. No thought-transports allowed for him. The journey wasn't quite over.

What looked like a vast abacus flat on its back sprawled before Hexipher suspended in an ocean of calm golden plasma. Not even with godlike senses could he peer beyond the plane this multiverse engine. Each row held millions of universes. Every rotating disc was an information-plate reminding Hexipher of ancient vinyl records in his true human life. In the middle of the dark plates, was a holographic sphere so dark that it ripped any rogue light away. Music of creation flowed from the rotating plate into the sphere as melodic code to program each universe. To the minds inside the spheres, some generated from within and others downloaded, the realities they inhabited were boundless and real as real could be. Hexipher knew better.

Hexipher had been many people, many genders, many forms, and even insects. All the inhabitants of the hub had been met except one. Hexipher could not see the others anymore in the hub though he sensed the billions of entities traversing and propagating through this Over-Reality. The entity he hadn't met terrified Hexipher more than going into a prison universe for thousands of reincarnations. He was guilty of acts that forced a part of his being to disengage and teach him the lessons he forgot. Sentient, sapient, and self-aware beings were not to be toyed with. They were not to be puppets and none were above the other in the end. Here before the expanse of the vault, a threat loomed.

A crease in the dark space above folded. A crackle of white light tore through and fused into a sphere. The false star sparked to frightening luminosity above the walkway. Hexipher shielded his sight. The deck of metallic honeycomb grating and the spans of amber guardrails took on a translucent phase transition.

Hexipher had never seen the planck do this before. The star lowered and a spotlight fell over Hexipher. The light pulsed three times and stopped. Before him appeared a massive seed wrapped in strands of fire. The Gardner was present.

"Nice to meet you," Hexipher said and bowed.

"Thought it was time after these eons and epochs. Seems we have a problem," the Gardner said and the words vibrated the decking below.

"Yes. I know that. What will be done? Exile? Erasure?"

"What have you done?"

"Feels like everything but I violated the rights of sentients by placing them in prison universes because I felt them a threat to my status as a Primus Inter Pares in my minor realm," Hexipher said.

"What did you learn from your insertions?"

"Hierarchies are artificial. Made from evolved social behavior that went out of balance. Useful constructs when in small groups are dedicated to specific tasks but not beneficial as operant modes of behavior of the entire group as it hinders ascension, progress, and betterment. It values the present structure over the future evolution. It becomes more important than the entities who are in it. I was a hierarchy unto myself."

"Well that is a mouthful. But you already knew that. What did you learn?"

"The minds in all the universes are important even if the realities are virtualities to me. To them, they are not. After living so many lives and doing almost everything, I took existence as granted," Hexipher said and felt something he had not in eons. Shame.

"Time to move on then and time is but a meager magician. Now you need to learn the tricks. Let's go," the Gardener said and they transported to a place Hexipher had never seen. The outside of the hub of 10 to the 20,000 of universes.

They stood on a curving plane of solid abyss. A horizon glowed like a titanic dawn of prismatic lights. To the right in what he could only fathom as a sky was a wormhole. To the left, the same. In between, a flow of objects. A quick scan of his memories and Hexipher found similar objects: neurotransmitters. Yet they glowed with internal energy and paused sometimes as if to watch what was going on.

"Are we inside some being's mind? Those look like synapses?"

"No, Hexipher. Take it all in," the Gardener said and a strand of fire made a hand and touched the center of the seed form. It became clear. They were on an object like the universe plates in the vaults. They were at waystation.

"I don't understand. Are those portals?"

"Knowing you don't understand is the first part of knowledge. Can you do it?"

"Do what?"

"Leave it all behind."

"Where do they go?"

"I don't know."

Leaving the memories, the abilities in the hub, and his ego for a moment felt too much to endure. Then, Hexipher leapt. Lilly petals filled the sky and ground below.

We all must move on.

Dolly 23

By

Joshua L. A. Jones

Edited by Mark C. Frankel

Dolly 23

The zombies were beautiful. Not what Shepherd expected at all. Perfect symmetry. Unblemished skin. Eyes glittering with silver metallic specks. The gossamer robes that draped over their toned bodies were beautiful too. The midday sun made the cloth appear like smoke curling around their frames while they ambled by in a perfect rhythm of footsteps.

Perhaps Advisor Remes was right? The video files in the Vault's archive were fiction and not fact. These creatures were not the decayed undead. They were unliving though, Shepherd thought.

Crouched in the reeds along the sandy bank of the river, Shepherd and Night scanned the line of zombies ambling down the gravel path toward the apple orchard. The icy water flowing from the mountain runoff chilled their feet, but Night couldn't feel it. The PM robot shifted from human form to panther-mode in a slow and methodical way that unnerved Shepherd. Polymer skin stretched on its face. Metal bones and plastic muscle detached and surged under the skin. Night bent down onto all fours as bronze pigments darkened to a deep gold to match the reeds.

"The ZB's have not noticed us," Night signaled to Shepherd's com-plant.

"They don't seem to notice much of anything, Night. We'll see what happens when they reach the grove and shut down after sunset," Shepherd replied through the com-plant.

The rows of zombies passed over a low berm and into a meadow dappled with white wildflowers. Shepherd and Night slunk out of the reeds and made their way up the bank. Being barefoot, Shepherd made no sound, but even the pebbles under foot were smooth from years of river erosion, they pressed on sensitive skin. Shepherd stopped and slung the hardcase backpack around. Night crept a bit closer to the gravel path that once must have been a logging road. The backpack opened with a click of the latch and Shepherd pulled out gel shoes. They slipped on and automatically formed to fit the damp feet. Three mosquitoes landed on Shepherd's arms and injected their mouthparts into the ochre colored skin. One second later, they shriveled up and fell to the ground dead.

Nasty little creatures, Shepherd thought.

Bending through the border trees along the meadow, they snuck in the shadows until they came across the apple orchard that spread between two foothills.

"Avalon Valley," Night said.

"I don't understand. This is where this cohort rests at night. They should be patrolling the zone," Shepherd said and pointed to a clearing in the verdant copse.

"Looks like the burial ground is closer than we thought. Bigger too. Almost fifty yards square," Night said and extended its telescope eyes.

Night scanned the exposed field between the trees hanging with ripe apples. The heat signatures of the ZB-zombies shifted from a cool blue to a blazing yellow with red heat flowing around their heads.

"Something is happening. Not normal photovoltaic absorption," Night said and retracted its eyes. Shepherd slung the backpack off their shoulders and pulled out a swathe of transparent cloth. The fibers seemed to catch the light and bent it around the length. A hood drooped down over Shepherd's forearm.

"Incognito mode time," Shepherd said, put the backpack on, and draped the hood over their head in one continuous motion. Then, Shepherd all but disappeared from the visual spectrum of light.

"Agreed," said Night and the pigments in its synthetic covering changed to a forest camouflage with patches of green and tan and gray.

They stalked down the valley and bounded from one apple tree trunk to the other. Though the gel shoes absorbed the impact and silenced most steps, the litter at the base of the trees was thick with sticks and twigs that cracked to announce their presence. A flash of white light spotted down from the sky. Too bright to be natural. They stopped thirty yards from the clearing. Night surveyed the sky and shook its head, an attempt to mimic human body language.

"Mirror drones," Night signaled to Shepherd's com-plants.

"Focusing the sun like an Archimedean mirror. That must take hundreds of drones," Shepherd signaled back.

"Thousands."

They watched as the zombies lined up in perfect rows and lifted their arms to the sky. An itch scrawled down Shepherd's back, but they resisted the urge to scratch. Taking off the backpack would create too much motion and the zombies were engaging in a new behavior.

Better to be still than risk some new sensory ability the zombies developed since the last satellite scan. Even with the mirage cloak, Shepherd thought.

The mirror drone's tightened formation above and the reflection focused as if through a giant lens. A static charge tickled through the air and blue arcs of electricity jumped from treetop to treetop. Shepherd's amber eyes shifted to ice blue.

"What in the universe is going on?" Shepherd signaled to Night through the com-plant.

"Energy to matter I suspect. Some quantum level alchemy," Night signaled back.

The zombies began to vibrate like a struck tuning fork. Shepherd squinted but zeroed their gaze on the closest zombie glimmering in the white light. The tips of the zombie's fingers began to transform. A film as dark as graphite coated the fingers and coursed over the arm. The smoky clothes adhered to the zombie's body as a bandage to staunch an open wound. The film covered the entire body in seconds. Standing straight and still like statues made of onyx, the zombies emitted a low frequency rumble Shepherd felt in the lower regions of their gut. And the gut did not like it.

"Do you sense Dolly 23?" Shepherd signaled to Night who was now crouched so low its belly brushed the ground.

"No, but that doesn't mean it isn't somewhere nearby in a shielded location," Night signaled back.

They both zoomed back their sight when the zombies began to sink into the dirt up to their knees. No need to watch further. They understood, in a limited way, what the zombies were doing by going into the ground.

"That's planting behavior. They only do that at night to share data. Not good," Shepherd signaled.

"That new form is not planting behavior," Night signaled back.

In a fast flip, Shepherd had the backpack out and unclicked the latch. A small ceramic cylinder with two blue buttons glowed. Night turned to investigate. It lifted off the ground and blinked its panther eyes. Shepherd pulled out the cylinder and then stuffed it under the mirage cloak.

"Put up your barrier. I'm going now," Shepherd signaled and launched toward the open field.

"No, stop," Night signaled but it was too late.

Shepherd thought about speed and amped up the adrenaline coursing through their veins. In a moment, it was hard for Night to track their movements. Shepherd's gel shoes dampened impact and muffled the noise. All that passed through the rows of zombies was a whirl of distorted hot air and then the cylinder seemingly came out of nowhere. Night got up its barrier just in time before an EM pulse shocked through the orchard.

Nothing.

The zombies did not fall but the white light from above faltered and died. Shepherd dropped the hood of the cloak and leaned close to examine a female zombie. She was as still as a ruined city.

Night came to the edge of the field and used its paw to call Shepherd back.

"It's okay. I think the EM pulse fried them," Shepherd said and flinched. A patter of sharp rain fell onto the cloak but there were no clouds in the sky when Shepherd looked up.

"Oh no," Shepherd said and started to run when a downpour of mirror drones the size of hornets pelted down. The edge of the field was close. A few more steps but Shepherd felt something grab their ankle and they tumbled down. Kicking back as hard as possible, Shepherd released the grip and scrambled away. A zombie was climbing out of the soil and clawed at Shepherd. The rest were doing the same.

Shepherd and Night fled. They hoped the intel they got on the zombies was true in at least this one case. They trampled the meadow leaving crushed white flower in their wake and barreled over the berm. Behind them a chant bellowed "Brains."

The river was close. The fresh scent wafted over the gravel road. Night looked back to see the zombies jogging toward them and gaining. A large gnarled piece of driftwood blocked Shepherd's path and they leapt over. They landed in a small pool filled with scummy water and fell flat. Night was at the river's edge and pointing back to the gravel path. The zombies were coming down the bank. Shepherd waved Night on and it ran into the water and sank below the current. Shepherd spun and sprinted to the river. All that was heard was "Brains" until the frigid water shocked Shepherd's ears.

Night was waiting for Shepherd on the far shore when they dragged themselves out of the rushing river. Panting and tired, Shepherd rolled onto their back.

"That was a mistake," Shepherd said.

"Yes, it certainly was," Night replied and transformed into a human form. Shepherd couldn't watch.

"The information on the zombies is incomplete. But at least the info on the water was right," Shepherd said and took a deep breath. Now standing up as a smooth bodied human, sans genitalia, Night pointed across the opposite shore. Shepherd bent up and looked. The zombies were gone.

"You should have waited until I did a proper scan of that coating material," Night said.

"I assumed they went into the dormant mode where they communicate. Thought we could end this mission early and get Dolly 23 back," Shepherd said when a creak started them both. Up on a low branch of an old elm, perched a figure all in black.

That can't be, Shepherd thought. No people were supposed to be in this region.

The figure swayed with the breeze and the black hooded robe flowed like raven's feathers. The fabric was iridescent and ate all the surrounding sunlight.

"Not communicating. Recharging. New adaption to let them work longer at night," the figure said and hopped down like a hawk.

"Who or what are you? Night asked and stood between Shepherd and the figure.

"Both are very good questions. My name is Hexipher. For now, but before it was something else. I think it was Horus or maybe Hero. I get the future and past mixed up," Hexipher said and popped down the hood to reveal a dark mane of silky blue hair and a male human face. But not entirely. He had owl eyes and an owl's stare.

Shepherd got up and looked the man up and down. Hexipher scratched his head and then looked at his fingertips as if expecting to see something but nothing was there.

"How do you know so much about the zombies?" Night asked.

"Zombies? Is that what they're calling them now," Hexipher replied and titled his chin up to face the sun.

"Answer the question," Shepherd said and stepped by Night.

"I know so much because I made them. Or I think I did," Hexipher said and closed his avian eyes.

"You couldn't have. They've wiped out everything years ago. Too long for you to have survived out here alone," Night said.

"They don't bother me. They already got the information in my brain. Nothing new here for them," he said and tapped his skull that made a clunking sound like it was made of tin and partially hollow.

"Perfect. Then you are going to help us get our sheep back," Shepherd said and stepped a foot closer.

"Sheep? That's crazy. Regular sheep don't exist anymore," Hexipher said and opened his eyes to stare with menace at Shepherd.

"This is a clone. A special clone," Night said.

"How special," Hexipher asked.

"Special enough so that if you don't help us, I'll lock you in a deep cold dungeon in the Rocky Mountains," Shepherd said.

"Sorry, nope. Can't help," Hexipher said and turned his back on them.

"It is a storage unit. The DNA is encoded with information that might help us take the world back," Night said. Hexipher spun back to face them.

"Data stored in DNA and not the brain implants? Interesting work around. I will help you. I'll help you by making sure you get to the Gulf of Mexico and get aboard the last barge to Niani. That is the only salvation. Escape," Hexipher said.

Shepherd leapt and grabbed Hexipher by the collar.

"No, I am a shepherd and I do not lose my flock," Shepherd said with a low grumble.

"Seems you already have," Hexipher said.

In the close woods, all the birds took flight from the trees. Crows cawed an alarm. Finches and sparrows flocked and flew away in spiraling formation. Night shifted its vision and peered into the woods looking for predators that filled the forests. Not one but twenty heat signatures glowed shuffling towards them in rows of five.

"They're here," Night said. Hexipher shook his head, "Always when I'm having fun."

A single scout zombie's face breached the shadows of the forest canopy then retreated. Shepherd hooked an arm around Hexipher's waist and lifted. Shock filled Shepherd's eyes.

"You weigh almost nothing. Makes this easier though," Shepherd said and bolted to the river. Night followed. Hexipher whistled a cheery tune until they dove under the surface. Holding onto Hexipher was difficult for Shepherd while doing a one-arm side stroke. The currents tugged at the man in the strange black robe. Night ran along the bottom of the river kicking up dirt and pebbles. Hexipher stuck his finger in his ear and twisted as if checking for wax as water surged over his face. The current was swift and brought them hundreds of yards down river when Night surfaced. Shepherd took a refreshing breath, but fear closed around their mind. On both sides of the river, zombies stood and watched them drift.

"They're flanking us. Keep going down river until I give the stop command," Shepherd signaled through the com-plant.

"Message received," Night signaled back.

"This river will merge downstream with another and flow flat into the gulf. You should really just go with the flow," Hexipher said and spit a stream of water from his thin lips.

"No, got to get Dolly 23 back. You are staying with us until then," Shepherd said and tightened their grip.

"Hostage situation? How boring. Fine, I'll help you get your sheep back. Not that it will save you," Hexipher said and the rush of the river grew louder.

"Rapids ahead," Night signaled to Shepherd.

Of course, Shepherd thought.

...

Battered and bruised from a few impacts with boulders lodged in the river, Shepherd made landfall with Hexipher in tow. Night rose out of the water like a slow-moving piston and walked the sandy shore strewn with debris to scout for enemies or traps. Hexipher plopped down on the small section of beach where a recent flood had cut through the slope to the forest. Exposed roots stuck out of the tiny cliff and stones spotted it like pimples.

The backpack was a bit wet but Shepherd wiped it off with the malfunctioning mirage cloak. Night came back and stood next to Hexipher with a watchful eye. Shepherd sat down facing the new member of their motley group and put a hard stare on him.

"Story time. Spit it out," Shepherd commanded. Hexipher tilted his chin down.

"Fine. Once upon a time, a man, me, wanted to help clean up the world. Climate change was being stabilized but not fast enough and we needed answers. Help. New nanotechnology was being advanced and humans could connect their thoughts. So, I thought to look to the wisdom of the crowd and pose a question. A thousand people signed up. Quickly we came up with new solutions to environmental disaster. I guess some people did not like this and set to break the chain of minds. An update to the nanobots created a hive mind. That was never supposed to happen but was reversible. But, something else slipped in. A primary command that overruled all. It was to collect data. All data. And send it to a repository. A couple greedy guys decided to hoard data and used others to do it. Problem was the coding conflicts. Error cascades. The guys were discovered but not before the melding. You know the rest. Infection. Exodus to the ocean. So on and so on," Hexipher said and tossed back his wet stringy hair.

"Are you still connected to them?" Night asked and crouched.

"In a way, yes."

"Can you search for our missing sheep?" Shepherd asked.

"Maybe. You won't reach it though if they have it stored near a planting field."

"Find it and we'll figure something out. And you'll be our guest," Shepherd said.

"Fine. You should really cut your losses and go to Niani. Would save time."

"Just do it," Night said. Hexipher shrugged and closed his eyes.

His eyes opened with a snap. "You're in luck. A communication node is nearby to the north-west. It let me gain better vision. Though I'm not certain it is your Dolly 23, but a few anomalous lifeforms are being held in a pen near the planting field just beyond. Not human. That's for sure. You know, I'm glad you are so determined. What an excellent test this will be," Hexipher said and collapsed to the ground. In a moment, he was sound asleep.

"We go at nightfall. We get in and get out. I won't make a mistake this time," Shepherd said. Night nodded once. They sat in the shade of an oak curved over the river. Mosquitoes died as they tried to suck Shepherd's blood.

As night drifted down, Hexipher slowly rose to consciousness. Night scanned the horizon and Shepherd rocked back and forth in a trance. Thoughts were sped up in Shepherd's mind. Visual simulations of the rescue ran over and over. Small variables led to drastically different outcomes. A deep yawn broke the trance and Shepherd saw Hexipher stretching his gangly arms over his odd shaped head.

Bird calls wove through the surrounding woods and gave Shepherd a sense of ease. Animals being around meant the zombies weren't. Clumps of wet sand dropped off Shepherd's knees as they stood up. A patch of dirt clung to Hexipher's face where it met the ground while he slept. He didn't bother to brush it off.

"Please wipe your face," Shepherd implored.

"Does that bother you?" Hexipher replied.

"Mirror neurons are burning. Been running sims of the rescue so my empathy mods are making me feel it just by looking at you," Shepherd said.

"Over-sharing. The source of the problem. It's all cyclical. In the past, the clutches of non-binary children were always so excellent at empathy. Glad to see that hasn't changed," Hexipher said and made his way to the river's edge. Shepherd felt a surge of spiky heat run down their spine. With a single bound, Shepherd was about to smack Hexipher. Night stepped in the way.

"Save your energy," Night said and went to Hexipher. He saw the PM robot saddle over and shrugged. Hexipher cleared the dirt from his face with a few flicks from the talon like fingers.

"Seems that Shepherd is a bit quick to anger. My test certainly revealed that," Hexipher said.

"It is unwise to test Shepherd. I am programmed for restraint with humans. They are not."

The last rays of the sun glanced over the curve of the horizon and darkness surged to take its place. They left the security of the river and trundled through the woods. When they reached a thinning copse, the bird calls were gone. The group stopped behind the last of the massive maples and Shepherd donned the mirage cloak. Night transformed into a panther and Hexipher yawned.

Behind a sheath of darkness that rippled and flowed like water, Shepherd poked out a hand from under the concealing sleeve.

"How far?" Shepherd asked and Hexipher scratched his head.

"Closer than you think," he said and pointed to a clearing that emitted a soft green glow.

"I sense the planting field just beyond this florest," Night said.

"That's what you call the modified florescent meadows? Neat. I called them Experiment Bio-Lumin 161115. A colleague recommended 'Torch Field' but I said they only glowed. Not burned. I like florest," Hexipher said. A blur of darkness flowed to Hexipher and Shepherd uncovered their face. There they were. Nose to nose.

"Do you ever shut up?" Shepherd said.

"Seems you failed this test too. Won't be able to help you if you continue this way."

"I don't give an erg about your tests," Shepherd said and popped the hood back.

"Excellent, passed that one," Hexipher said and began walking to the florest. He stopped and waved them on, "Don't worry. You're safe until the planting field."

The field was not far.

A small cylinder floated in the air. Night rotated its vision to infrared and scanned the field where the zombies were all planted up to their knees in the soil. No strange black coating that ate the sun. No motion. Just stillness from the zombies billeted in row after row. Under the soil, Night saw a heat signature of small tendrils squirmed along and connecting the zombies together. One after another, the tendrils crept and branched out to form a network.

"Put the cylinder away, Shepherd. They might see it," Night signals to Shepherds com-plant.

"Oh, sure," Shepherd signaled and the cylinder disappeared under the watery mirage of night.

"Better hurry before they link up and start chatting. I give you five minutes," Hexipher said.

"Going now," Shepherd signaled Night. The gel of Shepherd's shoes changed to dampen impact and sound.

Night could pick up on the few vibrations Shepherd gave off but Hexipher looked to his side as if to tell Shepherd something.

"Don't bother. Shepherd is gone."

"Oh, that camo-tech is better than what I had," Hexipher said and scratched his head.

"Those are nano-bot/fungus mycelium communication nets, aren't they?" Night asked with a low rumbling growl.

"Indeed."

"Vibration sensors?"

"Not when I made them. But things change."

The edge of the field was clear of undergrowth. Native grasses bordered but held back from the perfectly trimmed field. This reminded Shepherd of a VR golf course that the others played during rec-time.

Wonder how they keep this field so manicured, Shepherd thought and picked up the pace but not enough to disturb anything underfoot.

Midway, the cylinder appeared and began to sink into the ground. It was harder to peg in the dirt than Shepherd had thought but a few good twists did the job. A signal flowed between Shepherd's com-plant and the cylinder. The detonator went active. A simple thought would send an EM pulse first and then the explosive would make a crater of the whole field. Unless a jamming signal blocked it. Shepherd hoped there was no such interference and began to search for the pen.

The reason why the field was so manicured became apparent. Four aggressive little mower bots held guard around an animal pen. Saw blades hung from articulated swing arms above the boxy bodies half the size of Night. All splattered in green plant carnage, the metal bodies hummed. They were on but not active.

The pen was another problem. Thin posts were bound together with three levels of wire that crackled with electricity coming from a capacitor pylon in the center of the pen that looked like a willow tree sending its leaves out to the four corner posts. There were a couple problems to deal with but Dolly 23 was lying on a mat of straw next to the feeding trough. Dead rabbits littered the ground next to the wire fence. A llama paced back and forth and eyed where Shepherd was standing.

It can't see me, can it? Shepherd wondered.

Behind the pen, Shepherd pulled out the backpack. Inside was a coil of wire and cutters. Carefully, Shepherd trimmed off three lengths. The frayed edges curled into hooks with a signal sent from Shepherd's com-plant. Using the sleeves of the mirage cloak as gloves, Shepherd attached the wires in sloping curves on the electrified border levels to create a hoop big enough to get through. Another signal changed the properties of the meta-metal to be more conductive than the simple fencing. Shepherd tested the hopefully dead wire in the hoop with the cutters. No shock. No spark. No arc.

The wire right above the ground was the thickest and hardest to cut but it gave way with a bold snap. Shepherd scanned the area to see if the zombies have moved. They didn't but the llama began to bray and buck. This was not something Shepherd considered when entering the pen. The llama spat and charged. Shepherd rolled on the ground to avoid its stomping hooves and climbed next to Dolly 23. The sheep didn't move a muscle and its eyes were glazed as if drugged. The llama backed up and engaged in display attacks and reared back while making more of a commotion.

The last choice, Shepherd thought and pulled out a tiny dart from the mirage cloak sleeve pocket.

The dose was enough to kill Shepherd instantly. This was the last choice if ever caught by the zombies. Shepherd clicked the base and half the poison vial emptied into the ground. Then, with a flick. The llama spat, shook, and collapsed. The fall seemed to rouse the mower bots that began to spin their cutting wheels.

Dolly 23 was awake but wouldn't move. Shepherd grabbed tufts of wool and dragged Dolly 23 out through the gap. They would never make it out fast enough if Dolly 23 wouldn't follow on its own. That was the plan. No one had thought the zombies would drug an animal. Unless, they thought it was special or it was a trap. Breaking protocol, Shepherd signaled Night through the com-plant.

"It's a trap. Move back," Shepherd signaled.

"Four ZB's are shaking loose from the ground near you. Should I...?"

"No, disarm. Move back. Search and destroy later if necessary. Go," Shepherd said and saw the mowers ramp up. They clacked and buzzed their articulated arms. They moved slow but not slow enough. Shepherd lifted Dolly 23 and struggled to keep a grip. The native grasses were not hard going but it was not hard going for the mower bots either. Jogging wasn't in the picture so the sheep and the shepherd fast waddled through the woody underbrush that scratched Shepherd's legs, which healed almost in seconds. The mower bots began to cut away at the shrubs and saplings in their way. Heaving with harsh breaths, Shepherd made it to the forest border with thick deadfall and vines. The mowers gnawed at the vegetation as their blades whined and rattled. A large log covered in mushrooms and lichen and moss blocked Shepherd's path. Dolly 23 began to bleat when tossed over the dead tree. Shepherd hopped over, grabbed Dolly 23, draped the cloak over, and sent the signal.

The mower bots went silent. There was nothing but the wind until a white flash severed the darkness followed by a shockwave. Shepherd felt the dirt, sticks, and leaves rush over and then an impact. Everything that was so bright and white went pitch black.

Struggling to wake, Hexipher's face appeared in Shepherd's flickering vision. Dust cluttered eyelids tried to blink away the heavy call to sleep. The wide avian grin in Shepherd's narrow sight activated a Flight or Fight response. Hexipher puts his arms up to show he was no threat and backed away.

"Hold on, kid. It's all right."

"The zombies?"

"The ones over there are permanently off."

"Night?"

"Falling," Hexipher said and wrinkled his brow, "Oh, you mean the robot. It's fine. Right now it's searching the carnage. Better hurry up and get. The seared flesh will bring roving composter swarm puffballs."

Still shaken, a new question about puffballs had to be held for later, but one question had to be answered. Shepherd cleared away a layer of dirt and debris off the mound next to them. Dolly 23 was there. Breathing. Not moving otherwise. A com-plant signal was sent and Night was soon charging through the wastes of flattened trees and zombie bodies.

Traveling at night with Night hauling Dolly 23 strapped to its back was slow until they met back with the river. The wind spooked Shepherd when the branches and leaves seemed to almost rustle in a way that mirrored language. That's all I need, intelligent trees wanting to warn the zombies about us, Shepherd thought.

As if reading the thought, Hexipher chuckled and said, "They do speak. But at the roots. Fungus and soil and wood all sharing a chemical language too fast for us."

"I am aware of plants and chemical messaging. Here's the river coming up. The moon should help show the way," Shepherd said and looked up the gibbous moon. Down on the river, the moon's reflection rippled off of the river's surface. A celestial signal lamp caught in the current.

The silence of the next few hours told Shepherd they were still in dangerous territory. The river met a gradual slope and widened. The forest gave way to wetlands. The rocky and sandy riverbed fell away to spongy soil. Reeds and gnarled woody growths lined the banks of the river.

"The river is now only two meters deep. This will not stop the ZB's," Night said and they stopped on the last patch of dry dirt that formed a bridge between forest and saltmarsh.

"We're close to the place that has what we need," Hexipher said beckoning them to follow on a twisting path through the reeds.

Must be an animal path. Means there's life around but this is the wrong direction, Shepherd thought.

"Hold up. Wrong way. This leads south. We need to go west," Shepherd said.

"No. You need to go south."

"No, we need to get back to the Vault. That is west. That was our mission," Shepherd said.

"No. It wasn't. Going back was never in the plan," Hexipher grumbled.

Startled, confused, and a bit annoyed, Shepherd gulped down the brewing anger. Night's head rotated toward Hexipher like a wrench was torquing its neck.

"We are going back to the Vault," Shepherd said.

"You can't."

"No, we head west and will reach it," Shepherd said and watched a mosquito land on their hand. It died and dropped to the ground.

"You can most certainly head west but you will never reach the Vault."

"Are there dangers we were not informed about before we set off?" Night queried.

"Yes."

"Then we will go around them and reach the Vault," Shepherd said and fear traipsed down their spine when Hexipher shook his head.

"No. The Vault is gone. And before you get all doubtful and protest then make a stupid mistake, let me show you," Hexipher said and lifted his hands. The air around his fingers warped like molten glass.

Strange, Shepherd thought... until the signal filled their mind with a strange flipbook image creating a stuttered animation of Hexipher in long robes exiting the Vault's massive metal doors with Administrator Remes.

A fuzzy sound clicked a few times and the spade shaped face of Administrator Remes entered their minds. He looked younger, less wrinkles, and no dark circles under his amber eyes glared at them. Shepherd was almost uncomfortable with the face. They had only known the worn and perpetually irked expression of Administrator Remes. Then, his voice came.

"If you are hearing this, then we succeeded and failed. You are the last of the Shepherds and Poly-Morphs. Though I do not know what bio-stores are left, you must get them to the refuges on the sea. Only there can our coded data be put to use. Maybe one day, after the Zeno Barrier-intelligences either shutdown or transform into something else less hostile, all can come back. Until then, be safe our shepherd and lead your flock to safety." The voice crackled and the image faded like a shadow cast from a cloud.

In a single heartbeat, Shepherd was upon Hexipher with a twitching fist cocked back ready to strike. There was no retreat or resistance. Hexipher was still as a stone but had no weight to him. Night blinked once. Dolly 23 bleated a muffled and weak cry.

"A trick," passed through Shepherd's gritted teeth.

"No, the truth."

"How did you do that to me?" Night asked and shifted its back legs so Dolly 23 wouldn't slip off its back. The straps were loosening.

"I am a part of you both, in a way, so we are connected by com-plants just as I am connected somewhat with my mistakes. Since we don't have time, I was one of the people who started the Shepherd project as a last stitch effort to preserve what was left of diversity. Remes was my student. I can show you the destruction of the Vault and how it was overrun by zombies, or we can get out of here and save the data. By the itching of my fingers, something wicked this way lingers. Come on," Hexipher said and stomped down onto the swampy ground.

"What do you think, Night?" Shepherd signaled through the com-plant.

"He broke my security as if it wasn't there. I was not even aware of it. He must be telling the truth," Night signaled back and began to follow Hexipher through the reed path.

A good shepherd knows when to follow, when to lead, and when to corral, Shepherd thought and trudged through the spongey, muddy path.

At a bend where the river constricted a bit, Hexipher stopped and pointed to the moon but looked at the water. "Not good. Myco-Zeppelin. Guess we've walked enough in the marshlands to throw off the zombie from our trail. Hold on."

In the distance, Shepherd heard the far-off cries of gulls skittering through the sky. Then, an odd pumping noise. The thump-thump-thump transformed into a lower pitch and became a constant whine. A strange scent wafted by. Shepherd had never encountered such a scent and reluctantly thought of it as a fragrance. More of a nuisance and irritant.

"That would be burning hydro-carbons. Our ride is here," Hexipher said and waved over the murky river's edge by the muddy rim that separated the reeds from the slow-moving currents. A platform Shepherd identified as a boat with a flat keel, which looked like it would sink if Night got aboard. There were paddles on the deck and the gunwale was set with oarlocks covered in bird excrement. The bow was slightly raised but flat. Not like the images of canoes, rowboats, or ocean-going vessels Shepherd had stored in memory.

"This is the S.S. Exodus. Made it myself. Based on a bass fishing boat I had when I was a kid a hundred years ago," Hexipher said and slogged through the mud. He slid over the side and popped up to his feet. "Come on, it will hold us all. It's a special buoyancy material. Something you'll encounter more of on Niani."

The mud tried to hold onto Shepherd's gel shoes and each step forward made a slurp. Night fanned out its panther paws to make a mud version of snowshoes they had used hiking around the Vault under the last deep snow. The mud stank of sulfur and rot but they hauled onto the boat with not a peep from Dolly 23. Shepherd hoped it wasn't dying.

Just as Shepherd sat down to wipe the stinky mud off the gel shoes, Hexipher grabbed a pole jutting off a small outboard engine. With a twist, they were skimming over the river faster than Night could run. Hexipher looked back to the forest and then to Shepherd.

"Myco-Zeppelin will be on us soon. I jettisoned any active electronics. EM signatures will attract it. Well, not the thermal radiation from this motor but anything else," Hexipher said and forced a flat grin.

"Night and I are full of EM emitting elements. My mirage cloak will help me but Night?" Shepherd asked.

"I will leave Dolly 23 here and abandon ship," Night replied.

"No. Not acceptable. Will the Sludge work?" Shepherd asked Night.

"The radiation eating fungus from Chernobyl should mask my signature for a time but it is for you and only you," Night said and its paws began to twist in a way that was unnatural to release the straps that held Dolly 23 to its back.

"Nobody told me that. Anything else you are not telling me?"

"You know all you need to know."

"Just cover the PM in the goo but first cloak," Hexipher said and gunned the throttle. Shepherd pulled out the backpack and unlatched it.

All went well through the remaining evening. No sign of the Myco-Zeppelin trailing them or other hunter organisms. The Sludge seemed to work. According to Hexipher, there were only a few more kilometers to go but then they would need to hike some of the way. Soon, the sun rose with a golden glare so Shepherd shielded their eyes. Searching the distance in front of them was clear. This new clarity of sight shrunk hope when Shepherd surveyed the east. A globular mass hung in the sky like a sick cloud and was moving to intercept them.

"Is that a Myco-Zeppelin?" Shepherd asked and without looking Hexipher nodded.

A feeling of dread surged through Shepherd. Not wanting to look but needing to, weary eyes scanned to the western sky. Dread turned to crystalline fear, sharp and solid. Another mass was moving from the opposite direction that looked like a huge transparent heart pulsing with ill intent. The two would converge on the river delta where they would go ashore again.

"Another from the west. Not sure we can outrun them," Shepherd said and Night telescoped its neck to send an active scan.

"They know we're here, so I don't think the scan will give anything away," Night said and Hexipher nodded.

Dolly 23 perked up, scooted over to Shepherd, and nuzzled their arm. The backpack was on the deck and Dolly 23 sniffed it. Must be hungry, Shepherd thought and opened the pack. A sealed container of high-calorie kibble snapped open and Shepherd scooped out a handful for Dolly, who ate with a leisurely side to side chew.

The scan finished and Night retracted its neck. Dolly 23 snorted in disapproval.

"Options to evade are increasing speed, retreating, exit the boat and slog through the saltmarsh using the reeds and mud as cover," Shepherd said.

"The Exodus can't go any faster and time is limited. They are waiting for you but will not wait forever," Hexipher said and wiped away a strand of hair from his face.

"The Myco-Zeppelins use a siphon system like squid in the body of a jellyfish. This is how they fight the wind currents. If we could attack the sealing valve, they might fall to the ground," Night said.

"Could puncture those mushroom clouds with these paddles. If we could somehow make them projectiles," Shepherd said with hope on their breath.

"Mushroom clouds, huh? Certainly wish I had a couple of nukes around. Oh, sorry. Distracted again. They have stinger tendrils that snake through the air. They are thin filaments but strong mycelium. They shoot them to infect humans and turn them into zombies. Even if you puncture the beasts, a healing webbing would seal it in seconds," Hexipher said.

"One question. Hexipher, they won't let me onto Niani without certain precautions, will they?" Night asked.

"That is correct."

"The mention of nuclear weapons provides an option and so I have a solution that will speed up the boat, end the threat, and be myself," Night said.

Dolly 23 sniffed the air and let slip a baa of war. Shepherd rubbed their eyes and grimaced at Night.

"I don't understand," Shepherd said as the undulating living gas bladders loomed closer.

"Poly-Morph means I change. I choose to change before they change me," Night said and leapt out of the boat onto the flat sandy bank rounded with thick reeds swaying in the breeze.

Shepherd held out their hands and yelled, "No, get back here. You won't be able to draw them away with your EM signature." Hexipher cut the motor and they drifted. Night began to transform into its human form. Its head spun to gaze upon Shepherd.

"I am not drawing them. I am blowing them up. My power cell has one function you don't know about. Now let me be the hero," Night said and its hands flipped back and from the wrists metal rods pushed out.

"Hero, like the sound of that. Maybe one day I will be called that," Hexipher said and Shepherd hissed at him.

"Get back here now, I order you," Shepherd said in an even voice.

"Save them and goodbye," Night said and a static discharge railed in coils off its arms and beamed at the myco-zeppelins.

At first nothing happened when the streams of particles connected with the massive living balloons. The tendril coiled and electricity build up caused cloud to ground lightning. Night kept shooting and the clouds began to expand. The sun passing through the eastern myco-zeppelin bent as the large body distorted and became transparent as a lens. The bodies expanded and expanded and expanded. Night's beam weapon released the last of its charge and Night fell.

"Uh oh, might not have been enough..." Hexipher said but the myco-zeppelins burst into thousands of wispy strands like a spider web caught in a gale, "Nope, that did it."

A twist of the throttle and they were cruising down the shallow river. Shepherd stared at Dolly 23 and pet its soft curls of wool until they felt the boat come to ground. Hexipher got out and dragged the boat up a pebble strewn bank. The scent of brine mixed with the drafts flowing over the fresh water. The stench of the saltmarsh was gone. A hand reached over to Shepherd.

"Listen kid. We all make sacrifices," Hexipher said and Shepherd slapped his hand away.

"You sacrificed the world. You don't deserve to survive."

"Couldn't agree more. Listen, to get onto Niani all of those who could be infected with ZB nano-cells must be cleansed. Even though I don't think Night was infected, they would have done the process anyway and all Night was would be erased in the process. Same will happen in a way to me. They know what and who I am. You will be fine. So will Dolly," Hexipher said and presented his hand again. Shepherd took it and climbed out of the boat.

"Why?"

"You'll be fine because you are not walking around as a hive drone. If you were infected, it'd be obvious. The other why is more complicated and not for you to understand now."

"Will Dolly 23 make a difference on Niani?"

"All the difference. You take this sheep Little Bo Peep and walk straight to the dock at the end of this stream."

"How will I know I found the right people?"

"They were once shepherds like you. Go on, get. I got one more thing to do."

"How will you get there if we are leaving?"

"Got a way. Single person sleeper pod. I'll get fished out of the ocean and then go to sleep in the stasis vault. Come visit me if you want. I'll be in there for a long time. Maybe I'll be reborn when you're still alive and become a hero like your friend."

Dolly 23 snorted in displeasure while being hauled out of the boat and then again while being hauled back onto another. In what seemed like a blink, the sun set again and looming on the horizon was another frightful sight. The floating city of Niani.